No More Broken Promises

No More
Broken Promises

Angela Elwell Hunt

Tyndale House Publishers, Inc.
Wheaton, Illinois

Library of Congress Catalog Card Number 90-71568
ISBN 0-8423-0461-4
Copyright © 1991 by Angela Elwell Hunt
Front cover illustration copyright © 1991 by Ron Mazellan
All rights reserved
Printed in the United States of America

99 98 97 96 95 94
9   8   7   6   5   4

For Janet Williams

Important People in My Life

1. **Glen Perkins**, my dad. ♥♥♥♥♥
   A systems analyst at Kennedy Space Center, and
   my favorite singer. Handsome, even if balding.
2. **Claire Perkins**, my mom. ♥♥♥♥♥
   An interior decorator who works at home. "Cute"
   is a good word for Mom, even though she's older.
3. **Max Brian Perkins**, my brother. ♥♥♥♥♥
   What can you say about a little brother who's
   cute, smart, helpful, and never (well, almost
   never) a pest?
4. **Suki Buki Perkins**, my Chinese pug. ♥♥♥♥♥♥♥
   'Nuff said.
5. **Andrea Milford**, my best friend. ♥♥♥♥
   I'd give her five hearts, but I guess I should save
   those for family. She's cute, athletic, and better at
   almost everything than I am, but I like her anyway.
6. **Chip McKinnon**, the cutest guy in school. (♥♥♥♥♥)
   I have to give him secret hearts because no one
   can know how much I like him. And he's every
   girl's dream, so I don't stand a chance. But I can
   dream, can't I? (He gets five hearts because *if we
   get married someday, he'll be family, too.*)

1

"Class, put your books away. We're going outside now," Mrs. Hamilton commanded, but I didn't have a clue why she had suddenly ended her history lesson.

"What's going on?" Andrea whispered as she stuffed her books into the bottom of her desk.

"I don't know." I glanced around the room where Mrs. Hamilton stood and waited for us to file outside. "Maybe they were planning a fire drill, and the bell broke." Andrea giggled.

I never dreamed that January 28th would be the beginning of the end of life as I knew it. It had seemed like a perfectly normal morning at Astronaut Junior High School, except that it was colder than usual.

It is hardly ever cold in central Florida, but today we needed our jackets. Our jackets still looked new since we rarely wore them, and as

Andrea slipped into hers, I remembered her slipping into it a couple of weeks ago during the after-Christmas sale. "Oh, Cassie," she had gushed, "aren't these the best?"

That's my name, Cassie. Actually, it's really Cassiopeia . . . Cassiopeia Priscilla Perkins, to be exact. My dad is really into stars and astronomy—which is a good thing since he works at NASA—so he named me after the constellation Cassiopeia. Some people think it's kind of a strange name, and I agree, but what can you do about your name? I just ask everybody to call me Cassie.

Anyway, as I was saying, Andrea was real excited about the jackets when we tried them on. "That peach is just your color," she said, "and with my blonde hair, I'll look great in this blue one! We'll be alike, but different!"

So now we grabbed our great-looking, almost-matching jackets from the backs of our chairs and followed everyone else in the class out to the school yard. After we tiptoed past Mrs. Hamilton, Andrea giggled again. "Maybe it's a bomb scare or something. Can you imagine anyone wanting to bomb our school?" She shook her long hair and rolled her eyes at the thought. "Mom was working at the hospital once when they had a bomb scare, but she said no one left the building. They just kept to their stations while the police and their dogs searched everywhere."

Andrea has a tendency to exaggerate, so I

didn't argue. I didn't believe for one moment that *no one* would leave a hospital in a bomb scare. But Andrea's my best friend, and you've got to make some allowances for your best friend, right? Andrea and I have known each other since kindergarten, and her parents come over every weekend to play cards with my parents.

When we were younger, our moms signed us up together for piano lessons, ballet lessons, ice skating lessons, you name it. There we were, like peas in a pod, except Andrea always did well and I just tagged along. Like those old cartoons where Donald Duck dances and prances while his shadow just flip-flops along, we've always been together—Andrea shining in the spotlight and me following in the shadow.

We walked out onto the athletic field, the melting frost sticking to our shoes. *"Brrr,* it's too cold for me," I muttered, thrusting my hands deep into my pockets.

All of the other classes were spilling out, too, and we saw my brother, Max, standing on the other side of the field. He thinks he ought to be in eighth grade with me because he's a super-genius, but my parents knew I needed my own space, thank goodness. So they let Max test out of two grades, and now he's the only nine-year-old at Astronaut Junior High. He's probably the only nine-year-old in any junior high school in Florida, for that matter.

Max is all right for a kid brother. He can be a

pain like anyone else, sure, but he's never really been a pest like Andrea's brother, Jeremy. I've developed my own theory—little kids are pests only when they're bored. Max is never bored. He's too busy experimenting with his microscope and developing his ant colony to do goofy things like hiding spiders in my room or eavesdropping on my phone conversations. Jeremy can be a genuine pain in the neck, but Max is OK. I have to admit it's nice having a genius in the house because he helps me with things I despise like geometry, logarithms, and bug collections for science class. Max would rather do a geometry problem than eat, unless you're offering a Twinkie.

All the other sixth graders were running around, exercising their right to be hyper, but Max was looking intently at the sky. From where I stood he didn't look like a brain—with his hands in his sweater pockets and that concentrated expression on his face, he looked like a dreamy kid who would give anything to escape and go fly a kite. He has my mother's brown hair, which, thanks to a couple of cowlicks, always looks slightly windblown. But when you talk to Max, you can tell from his eyes that he knows more intellectual stuff than you ever will. Sometimes I wonder how Mom and Dad tell him anything. I suppose he realizes they know more than he does in terms of practical experience, but he'll catch up to them soon. It's only a matter of time.

10

Andrea and I walked over to say hello.

"Hey, Max, what's up?" I asked.

"The space shuttle," he said simply, and once again I felt like an idiot. Space shuttle launches didn't make headlines like they used to, now that we were used to them, but this flight had a teacher on it. No wonder the school had let us out to watch.

"Of course, that's why we're out here!" Andrea said, knocking the side of her head with her fist. "I love it! If this launch is delayed like all the others, we'll be out here for at least half an hour before the teachers give up and make us go back in."

"The flight has already been delayed twice in two days," Max explained patiently. "Dad said last night that NASA's under pressure to have a 'go' today. They'll probably launch if the winds aren't too strong."

Max wants to be an astronaut on the space shuttle someday. In fact, he'll probably submit his application for the next civilian flight. They've already invited a congressman, a schoolteacher, and a journalist to fly along; the minute they ask for nine-year-old whiz kids, Max will be at NASA's front door, I know it.

Dad is a systems analyst for NASA, which means he sits around at work discussing what went wrong when and why, and how it can be fixed. He must be good at what he does because something is always going wrong with one thing or another, and he's always being paged on his beeper. Even when he's at home, he's fooling around on his computer or working on mathematical problems that would turn my brain to mush. Max works right along beside him, and if Dad couldn't help Max get his foot in the door and his rear in a rocket ship, I don't know who could.

"Hey, isn't this the flight with the teacher on it?" Andrea asked. "Wouldn't it be hilarious if Mrs. Hamilton had been picked to go on the flight? Can't you just see her broadcasting our history lessons from space?"

"I can hear her now," I laughed, pinching my nose to make my voice as nasal as Mrs. Hamilton's: "Class, your attention, please. Andrea Milburn, stop whispering! Cassie Perkins, sit up and try to insert this into your brain! Those who do not learn from history are condemned to repeat it!"

Just then a whistle blew and a teacher who had been listening to his transistor radio began the countdown for us. Everyone picked up the chant; there's just something about a rocket launch that pulls at your stomach. Though I've been watching them from my front yard for years, I still get excited during the countdown.

"Ten!"

"Nine!"

"Eight!"

"Seven!"

"Six!"

"Five!"

"Four!"

"Three!"

"Two!"

"Ignition!"

"Blast-off!"

We stretched our necks and looked through the clear sky toward the east. I've seen launches from the VIP stands when my dad got us visitor's passes, and when you're that close you can see "USA" proudly written on the side of the ship and the shuttle as it rides alongside the huge rocket booster. But even from school we could pick out the white specks that were the rockets and the vapor trails that follow behind and gradually mushroom into the sky.

"There it is!" we all shouted as it began to climb from the horizon. "Time for the rollover," mumbled Max, who had been watching the second hand on his watch, and suddenly there was an unexpected puff in the sky. What should have been a single streak of vapor instantly became a crisscross of white and a pillow of fog.

I turned to Max and saw that his eyes were wide. "What happened?" I asked.

Max shook his head in disbelief, and the noise of the lift-off finally began to reach us. We heard and felt beneath our feet the familiar gentle and increasing rumble caused by the ignition, but when the vibrations should have faded, suddenly we felt, heard . . . and realized the horrible truth: the rocket and the space shuttle *Challenger* had exploded.

All around us the other kids knew something had gone wrong, but we weren't prepared for the shocked faces of our teachers. Mrs. Hamilton had bragged about submitting an application to ride the shuttle, and when she suddenly lost interest when Christa McAuliffe was chosen, I figured she was secretly jealous. But now we all stood in shock and horror.

Some of the younger kids began crying, and I saw teachers click into their automatic *"Shhhhh"* mode to quiet them down. But I remembered something else—

"Max—," I said, putting my hands on his shoulders and trying to make him take his eyes off the sky. "Max, is Dad all right? Did the shuttle blow up the Space Center too? Could the pieces fall on the crowds or on the building where Dad works? Will Dad be all right?"

Max just looked at me. "I don't know, Cassie," he said, a tear gleaming in the corner of his eye. "This isn't 'posed to be happening."

The teachers wasted no time herding us back into the classroom once the first shock had passed. Mrs. Hamilton dug in her file cabinet and passed out a dittoed worksheet—busy work—but we didn't want to do it any more than she wanted to teach. Nobody wanted to do anything. Finally our principal's voice came over the intercom:

"May I have your attention please."

For once, the room was already quiet.

"We have just learned that the space shuttle

Challenger has exploded at Cape Kennedy. The seven astronauts are missing. No one else was injured. A school counselor will be available if any student wishes to talk about today's incident; just make an appointment in the office."

After lunch, kids started disappearing from our classes. I knew their parents were picking them up and taking them home because the rest of this day was going to be a colossal waste. I knew Mom wouldn't come to get me or Max. She was an interior decorator and ran her business from home, and most likely she hadn't been near a television or a radio all day.

Everyone was totally zonked by what had happened. My fourth-, fifth-, and sixth-period teachers gave us study periods instead of teaching, then they sat silently behind their desks staring at us or their gradebooks.

For the first time I could remember, the bus ride home was quiet. There were some goofheads in the back who kept squealing, "*Kaboom!* Did you ever see anything so awesome?" Most of us, though, weren't thinking about the explosion but about the astronauts and that poor teacher. Max had a picture of the *Challenger* crew posted in his room, and he had even written a letter to Christa McAuliffe asking for a personal report on her trip when she returned. He had been so sure she'd write back. Now she wouldn't.

Mom met us at the door when we got home, which was unusual, and she asked gently, "Did you have a good day?" It was a dumb question, but I gave the regulation answer: "Sure, Mom. Have you heard from Dad?"

"Dad won't be home until very late," Mom called as she walked to the kitchen, her short brown hair swinging in time to her step. "He called right after the accident and said things were going to be horrible for a while. People are going to say the most awful things. . . ."

Max went straight to his room; I stood in the kitchen doorway and whistled for Suki, my pet Chinese pug. At least Suki wouldn't be bothered by the day's tragedy. Something had to be normal in our house today.

Sure enough, Suki came trotting into the room, panting from exertion and overweight. When she was a puppy, Suki had been long-legged and playful, but now she was eight—fifty-six in dog years. She panted constantly, ate too much, and drooled on occasion, but I didn't care. She was the best dog I'd ever seen.

Suki stood at my feet and looked up for some attention. I patted her head and together we walked into the kitchen just in time to see Mom reach into the freezer for a frozen dinner. Between her business, her women's club, and her aerobics classes, Mom never had time to cook.

"Imagine, your father was crying on the phone," she said quietly, not caring if I heard her or not. "I haven't heard him cry in years. But he was crying."

She popped the cardboard lid off a tray of frozen salisbury steaks and automatically slid it into the oven. I knew that next she would boil water for tea, then chop up some vegetable for dinner. When that was done, she'd sit down with the paper and wait for the oven timer to buzz.

I didn't want to watch her boil and chop and wait. I didn't understand how she could be so normal. The shuttle had exploded! Right in front of my eyes! Right where Dad was working!

But worst of all, my dad was crying. He was OK, and that was a relief, but he was crying. That was terrible.

2

Dad got all of us passes to the memorial service for the astronauts. Mom put on her best dress and brought out her one and only hat, a navy blue wide-brimmed number with a white bow. "Very chic," she said, looking at herself in the mirror. "And yet serious. Perfect for a funeral."

Max put on a dress shirt and a tie, and I searched my closet for something that looked as serious as Mom's hat. I could forget chic—nothing in my closet would come close to that description. But I didn't know if I had anything "perfect for a funeral." I'd never been to one, and I wasn't quite sure what to expect. But President Reagan was going to be at this memorial service, and something told me that Mom was right—a serious outfit was definitely called for.

I finally pulled on a white blouse and dark skirt,

but it didn't really matter because we sat way in the back of the crowd. All I could see were the backs of about a thousand black suits and a couple hundred television cameras. The families of the astronauts were in the front, right next to the president, but I didn't envy them one bit. How horrible to have someone in your family get up, kiss you good-bye, and never come home. I didn't know how they could handle it.

I do remember one line the president said. He said the seven astronauts had "slipped the surly bonds of earth to touch the face of God." Had they really? While he went on talking, I sat in my metal chair, uncomfortable in the sun, and thought about what it would be like to be with God. Were the astronauts with God just because they literally flew up into heaven, or were they there because they had given their lives for their country?

What would it be like to touch the face of God? Would it be as exciting as falling in love? Probably. As getting your heart's deepest desire? Possibly, but I guess that depended on what your heart's deepest desire was.

I couldn't help frowning. If being with God meant having to fly into heaven or give my life for my country, I wasn't sure I could pay the price. No one at the memorial service looked glad about the astronauts being with God. Everyone, from the reporters to the other families of NASA workers, looked serious and sad.

I could understand why. Even though it might

be comforting to think that my dad was talking to God, if he had been killed in the accident, I wouldn't be happy, either. The sadness in the air was so thick that I began to feel like I had lost someone, too. When the service was over and we turned to leave, I reached out and held my dad's hand just to be sure he was there.

That night I sat on our front porch and watched the sunset. I could hear the drone of the television from the living room where Mom was watching, and every once in a while I could hear Dad and Max yelp when one of them scored on their latest computer game. I wanted to be alone.

Suki was with me, though, and so was my private notebook. I've been keeping one since fifth grade, and in it I write my most private thoughts. It's not a diary, really, but instead a collection of my dreams, poems, and the words of songs I like to sing.

I wanted to write something for the astronauts. Once when I was in fifth grade, Beth Miller's dad died of a heart attack while he was sitting in his easy chair. In Mr. Miller's honor, I wrote a poem about a man who died, and my teacher liked it but said I shouldn't show it to Beth so she wouldn't be upset. So I didn't.

So even though I knew I'd probably never show it to anyone, I tried to write something to describe what I was feeling for the astronauts:

The early twilight settles around the world—
The silv'ry hush wraps itself around the earth.
I sit missing you.
The morning rain steadily drips from rooftops.
The buzz of the cricket adds to morning song.
My heart sings of you.
The cool evening breeze fingers my hair and cheek,
The sweet day is closing and nighttime has come.
But you are not home.
—Cassie Perkins, age 13.

It didn't rhyme, but the syllables matched up. Besides, it was all there, the loneliness, the sadness, the ache, and the love. If I were an astronaut's kid, that's what I'd be feeling.

I closed my book and whistled softly for Suki. As we went inside, I was really glad I hadn't lost *my* father.

After the initial shock of what they were calling "the *Challenger* disaster," things at school settled back into the usual routine. Mrs. Hamilton and the other teachers tried to carry on as usual, and Andrea kept trying to get me to look at Chip McKinnon, the cutest and most popular guy in the entire eighth grade.

But I had something else on my mind. More than anything else in the world, I wanted this year to be the time when I, Cassie Perkins, made my statement. I wanted the world to recognize my hidden talent. I wanted to be a singer, a star! I really can sing, although no one knows it but Max, Suki, and me.

I think I get my voice from Dad, who's a good Irish tenor. When I was little he used to sing "My Wild Irish Rose" as a lullaby, and I grew up wanting to sing like him. Now I want to sing like Mariah Carey. When I'm alone I practice singing songs along with the radio. Suki always looks up at me with her bulging brown eyes and tries to "yip, yip, yip" along.

One day I was alone in the house belting out a Whitney Houston song when Max appeared from out of nowhere. He was covered in dark sand, and I knew he'd been digging for bugs or something in Mom's flower bed. He had probably heard me singing through the open window, but I tried to pretend that I hadn't been doing anything important.

"Mom's going to kill you if you don't stay out of her flower bed," I warned.

"There's a new ant hill there," Max said simply, as if that made everything all right. "And by the way, your singing"—I braced myself for the worst blow a little brother could dish out—"is pretty good. You could sing on television."

I wanted to kiss him, but I threw a towel at him instead. "Clean up, and make sure you don't bring any of those disgusting ants inside."

I never seriously thought about singing until we read a poem in English class about a quiet Quaker girl who secretly wanted to be a scarlet Spanish Dancer. Mrs. Williams explained that the girl wasn't content to be a mild-mannered Quaker because she had the heart of a dancer. As I listened, I knew that poem applied to me. I have the heart of a performer, too.

Our homework for English was to write an essay or poem about our ambition. I knew most of the kids were writing about "I want to be a doctor" or "I want to be a computer programmer." But that scarlet dancer in the poem had done something to my imagination. The words flew out of my brain and onto my notebook paper:

> Outside dark rain is falling,
> Outside the wind is calling,
> Outside are people mauling,
> Falling down.
> Inside the lights are shining,
> Inside are lovers pining,
> Inside their souls are dining
> On the sound.
> The scarlet singer is a captor
>
> Who leads their minds to rapture,
> Who inspires their hearts to laughter
> By her song.
> Her gift was so long hidden,
> For years it went unbidden,
> They are sad it was so hidden
> For so long.
>
> "No more," she sings, "No longer,
> For now I am much stronger,

I will hide myself no longer,
In disguise.
Opportunity, I'll chance it!
If I hear a tune, I'll dance it!
If fear rears its head, I'll lance it!
World, surprise!"

Just like the Quaker maiden wanted to dance, I wanted to sing! Really sing! I'd been the quiet, ordinary maiden and Andrea's shadow for long enough, and I wanted to be something I knew I could be but I'd never been: a singer! In front of thousands of cheering people, in a sequined dress with spangly earrings, I wanted to sing! And Mr. Williams, our school's choir director, just might make it possible.

Every year our local high school performs a Broadway musical. Last year they did *West Side Story*, and the year before that they did *Oliver*, but this year they're going to do *Oklahoma!* Of course, the show isn't exactly Broadway quality, but all in all it's pretty good.

During our "Welcome to Second Semester" school assembly, Mr. Williams stood. "Now we all know Astronaut Junior High is the best, don't we?"

Everyone roared in agreement. Mr. Williams was OK and everyone liked him. "But each year," he went on, "it's Astronaut High School that gets all the attention and community support by putting on a major musical."

We answered with a universal "Boooooo!"

25

He smiled. "It's time our school did something to compete with them. Now, we can't compete with their budget, stage, and costumes, that's a fact. So we can't put on a full play—but don't we have as much talent as they do?"

Cheers.

"Don't we have as much support?"

More cheers.

"Can't we do just as good a job?"

The roof was about to come off.

Finally he gave us his plan: "We are going to learn all the music to *Oklahoma!* and we're going to perform it for our parents at the end-of-the-year concert. We're going to wear costumes and stage certain parts of the production—and everyone in school is invited to audition for a role."

That was it. After all that hype everyone— even the too-cool-to-be-a-fool kids—wanted to be in the play. For me, the play became my goal, my dream, and my deepest desire for my last year at Astronaut Junior High. I wasn't going to bother with cheerleading or academics or student government. I was determined to sing the part of Laurie in *Oklahoma!*. Everyone would be so surprised and amazed that ordinary Cassie Perkins could really belt out a song! I would go into high school with an amazing reputation, and I might even be invited to sing "The Star Spangled Banner" before all the home football games.

I kept my big plan a secret from everyone

except Max. I simply had to tell someone, and I had a sneaky feeling I couldn't trust Andrea with a secret like this. Knowing Andrea, if she thought singing the role of Laurie was a good idea, she'd start practicing and take the part right out from under me. So I didn't tell her, but one afternoon after school I knocked on Max's door.

"You can't come in," Max called. "I'm in the middle of an experiment."

I was prepared. "I have Twinkies."

Max would do anything for a Hostess Twinkie. Somehow he has the misguided idea that Twinkies are brain food.

"OK," called Max. "Come in quickly and try not to let too much sunlight in with you."

That request wasn't too far out for Max, so I slipped into the room and tossed the Twinkies onto his bed. Max was sitting on the floor dressed in his "scientist's outfit," an old white lab coat of Dad's. In the closet, under a fluorescent light, was Max's latest experiment: laboratory beakers filled with green slime.

"What are you doing now?" I asked.

"I'm growing algae in a controlled environment," Max replied, rubbing his nose in concentration. "I have to find the optimum growing conditions before I spin it into a powder and harvest the algae."

"Harvest it?" I asked, making a face. "Why would you want to harvest it?"

"To feed it to them," Max pointed at Jessica

and Jericho, his two pet gerbils. "You see, algae is very nutritious, and if they eat an enhanced diet they will produce more offspring at an advanced rate. Hypothetically, anyway. I'll soon have gerbils reproducing at unequalled rates, and I'll be able to populate Brevard County with gerbils in approximately 2.5 years."

"That's crazy, Max."

"No, it's not. Did you know the entire United States population of gerbils has sprung from twenty gerbils brought over in 1954 by Victor Schwentker?"

"Max," I stretched out over his bed and peered down at him, "there are enough gerbils in the world already. There are enough gerbils in Brevard County already. There are enough gerbils in this house already! We don't need more gerbils!"

"I know," sighed Max. "That's a problem. But advanced reproduction is only one possible result. The algae could make them healthier, more intelligent, and it could be more cost-efficient to eat algae than gerbil food. If algae is good food, just think—we could feed millions by harvesting it!"

"Millions of gerbils or millions of people?" I wrinkled my nose. "Anyway, you don't need a scientific experiment to prove it's good for you. I'm sure it is. It's gross and green, and generally anything that is green and gross is good for you."

"No." Max shook his head, absorbed in his work. "That's not true."

"Oh yeah? Name one thing that's gross and green and *not* good for you. Broccoli is, and spinach, and green beans, and asparagus, and . . ."

"Nasal secretions." Max dipped his finger in an algae-filled beaker and held it up under the light. "Especially when you've got a really bad cold."

Gross! The things he could come up with! "That's barfy, Max. I ought to get out of here before you totally make me sick."

"You should, but you won't." He grinned. "You had a reason for coming in here and bringing the Twinkies. What's up?"

Now was my chance. "Max, do you want to know a secret? Guess what I want to do!"

"Have a slumber party?"

"No."

"Pass history?"

"No. That's nearly hopeless."

"Meet Chip McKinnon at the movies?"

"That's my second greatest dream."

He looked at me. "Have Dad come home from work on time for a change?"

"No, although that would be nice."

"I give up. What do you want to do?"

I took a deep breath. "I want to sing the solo part of Laurie in our school's *Oklahoma!* production."

Max nodded, disappointed, no doubt, that I didn't want to build an atom bomb in the garage. "You could do it. The odds are pretty good."

"And I want to surprise everyone, especially Mom and Dad. You won't tell, will you?"

"Of course not."
"You promise?"
"I promise."
I grinned. The smiling, scarlet dancer was going to break out of her mold!

3

Since the *Challenger* disaster, Dad hadn't been home from work at dinnertime, and we hardly saw him at all. When he did come home, he'd take his foil-wrapped dinner from the oven and sit on a kitchen barstool and eat alone. Dad was very quiet these days, and we understood that the situation at NASA was not good. Everyone was trying to blame everyone else, and the systems analysts like Dad were going crazy analyzing what went wrong where, when, and why. Dad was also worried about those who worked under him. It was not a good time.

One night Dad didn't come home until midnight. The sharp click of the key turning in the lock woke me up, as if I had been waiting for it. I glanced at the clock and turned to go back to sleep, but my mother's sharp voice cracked right through my closed door.

"This has gone on long enough!" she snapped. "This is a family, and we don't see you anymore. You don't care to be with us, and you're using this *Challenger* thing as an excuse to pull away from us. The neighbors are beginning to talk! If you're not going to be a part of this family, why bother coming home at all?"

Dad's voice was muffled at first, as if he was trying to get out of the argument, but when Mom kept on yelling, his voice clipped through the quiet. "How can I come home to you when all you've cared about for years is your latest client and your circle of friends? We've grown apart, Claire, and I don't know if we can ever grow together again. This problem at work has nothing to do with us. I know we've stayed together for the sake of the children—"

"The children!" shrieked Mother. "You can't care about the children! You never spend any time with them!" As she went on in a tirade against my father, I covered my head with my quilt. A hot tear dripped down my nose, and I wondered if Max was awake.

They must have called a momentary truce because I heard footsteps coming down the hall. Someone opened the door to Max's room and peeked in, then I heard my door click and swing open. Suki, who had been sleeping at the foot of my bed, woke, and I felt her raise her head. I closed my eyes and pretended to sleep, but in the pit of my stomach I had the horrible feeling that nothing in our family was quite as it should be.

Would it ever be again?

I thought I'd feel better in the reality of daylight, but I woke up with a headache and a burning throat. "Oh no!" I whispered, straining to swallow. "The auditions are today and my throat hurts too much to sing! I'm going to miss the audition!"

I had a major fever, too, but I forced myself to get up and go to the kitchen for some orange juice. Maybe that would help. Max was already at the kitchen bar dunking his breakfast Twinkie in milk.

"You look like you were run over by a moon rover," he joked.

I gave him a withering smile and whispered, "Throat hurts. Auditions today. Can't make it."

If there's anything Max loves, it's a challenge, and he stopped chewing long enough to give me a triumphant smile. "I can fix that!" he said, his eyes gleaming. "Just let me mix you up a batch of my throat relaxer with vitamins. You'll feel great in no time."

"What's in it?" I was suspicious. "Algae?"

"No." Max grinned. "Although a good dose of algae would probably do you good. It's made of honey and oranges and lemon juice. If you drink it right before you sing, your throat will feel fine."

"The auditions aren't until three o'clock," I

reminded him. "I can't carry that stuff around all day."

"No problem," said Doctor Max as he put his breakfast bowl in the sink. "I'll rush home on my bike and mix up a batch and bring it to you. Just stall your audition as long as you can. Where should I meet you?"

I thought a moment. "By my locker. I can't be gulping strange stuff in front of everybody."

Despite my throat and fever, I was beginning to feel hopeful. "Just one thing, Max," I croaked as I turned to leave. "Could you make one of your inventions taste good for a change?"

I suffered through school. Andrea noticed my condition and couldn't believe that on the one day I really had a good excuse to stay home, I was crazy enough to come to school. But she didn't know about the auditions.

I was not only sick, I was more nervous than I had ever been in my life. I had never sung in front of people, and the thought of actually doing it was enough to make my heart pound. In English I sat and watched my locket actually *thump-thump-thump* against my chest. If I didn't die from drinking Max's potion, I'd probably keel over from heart failure.

At five minutes till three I leaned against my locker, quiet and miserable. All I had to do was shine through one song, maybe two, and then I could go home and quietly expire on my bed. I wanted to die under the covers and stay there for a week. Nothing, good or bad, could bring me out until I felt better. Mom and Dad could argue, I could win the part, the whole world could blow up, but I wouldn't care. I was too sick.

But where was Max? My throat still felt horrible, and it took a huge effort just to swallow. My nerves made my mouth so dry I could have drunk anything with pleasure, but there was no sign of any magic potion. At three o'clock I wanted to kill him. He promised to help me, and in a pinch he didn't even bother to show up.

I went on to the auditions without Max and his potion and smiled at Mr. Williams, who gave me a slip of paper with a number on it. Number 13. Great. Just what I needed for good luck.

The room was filled with hopeful Lauries and Curleys and Juds. Everyone wanted to be the lead singer, but I was at the point where I didn't even care. I slumped into a chair in the back of the room, closed my eyes, and hoped it would all end quickly.

But when my number was called, I cared. Somehow I got through "Oh, What a Beautiful Morning" without sounding too weak or too soft or too melodramatic. Mr. Williams looked up, surprised, and I smiled at him as I sang. No one knew it, but I deserved an award for my acting even in the audition.

When I finished, everyone clapped, but my ears were ringing so badly that I could hardly hear. On legs that felt like rubber I walked over to Mr. Williams. "Fine job, Cassie," he said and reminded me that the names of those selected would be posted within a week. I was free to go.

As I picked up my books and turned to leave, the choir room door opened and in burst Max, proudly carrying a beaker of gooey green liquid. "It's perfect!" he announced with the glee of a mad scientist, but I walked right past him.

"Nice going, Einstein," I muttered. "Your promises are really worth a lot."

4

The notices were posted on Friday afternoon, and I couldn't believe my eyes when I read, "Cassie Perkins—Laurie." Andrea couldn't believe it when she read "Chip McKinnon—Curley."

"Cassie Perkins, I can't believe you'll be singing love songs to the cutest guy in school!" she exclaimed. "And I really can't believe you didn't tell me you were going to audition. If I had known Chip was going to play the part of Curley, I'd have sung, danced, and stood on my head!"

I know, I thought. *That's why I didn't tell you.* Why do best friends like to compete so much? But it didn't matter. I wanted to play Laurie because I wanted to sing. Andrea wanted to play Laurie so she could gaze into the eyes of Chip McKinnon and sing, "People will say we're in love." That's the difference between us.

37

We hurried to the choir room where Mr. Williams gave me a musical score and explained that rehearsals would be three times a week after school. Everything had to be memorized by March because we were going to stage parts of the program, which would be performed in May.

"Stage it?" Chip McKinnon walked into Mr. Williams' office and Andrea dropped her jaw and gaped. "I thought we weren't going to have a stage."

"We aren't," explained Mr. Williams, handing Chip a score, "but as we sing it, those of you who have solos will move about and act out certain parts of the songs. It would be awfully boring to see you simply stand there and sing without any emotion or action. We might even try to add a little square dancing."

Chip made a face, and I had to giggle. Square dancing was obviously something Chip McKinnon didn't want to do, but when I thought about dancing with Chip I have to admit my stomach did a little flip-flop. Not because I had a crush on him or anything, but because I was afraid my feet would get tangled and I'd fall on my face in front of him. Besides, who will listen to you sing if they're too busy laughing at your clumsiness?

"Square dancing?" crooned Andrea, still gazing at Chip. "Mr. Williams, I've been a square dancer for years. I could teach Chip—and anyone else—in no time at all. "

"Then perhaps we can use you." Mr. Williams smiled. I could tell by his raised eyebrow that even he noticed Andrea's downright obvious interest in our production's leading man.

Chip *is* really interesting-looking. I'm not the type to get all mushy about television stars or athletic hunks, but I'll admit Chip deserves a second look. He has clear blue eyes, a quick smile, and hair the color of cornsilk. He is tall and thin, probably a future basketball player, and objectively speaking, I think we will make an attractive couple as Laurie and Curley if only because opposites are interesting. He's tall, I'm short. He's probably descended from some Swedish king, and I'm so dark my dad has always called me his "gypsy girl." In any case, I knew I'd enjoy the afternoon rehearsals—if Andrea stayed an arm's length away.

I'd rather be at school than at home anyway. I had not been on speaking terms with Max ever since he broke his promise to me. He apologized the afternoon of the auditions, over and over again, but I was too sick to even listen to him. I felt horrible that day, sick and tired and grumpy.

But when I told Max I got the part I wanted, he was glad to hear it. "That's great," he said simply. "I knew you could do it. So since you didn't need my throat potion to get the part, are you still going to be mad at me?"

"Yes, I am." I was over my sore throat, but I was still indignant that I'd been stood up by my little brother. "It's the principle of the thing. You made a promise to me and you broke it. You shouldn't make a promise if you can't keep it."

Max just rolled his eyes and went back into his room. Later I heard his computer keys clicking, and I knew he was engrossed in one project or another. He wouldn't let my little grudge upset him, but I wanted to stretch out my anger as long as I could. Sometimes there's something about being mad that just feels good.

There was a lot of anger in our house, but it was mostly felt and not heard. I was mad at Max and Max was mad at Mom because Mom was mad at Dad because he wasn't around much at all. Mom was wondering what the neighbors would think. And even though she didn't say much about Dad or her feelings, she exploded about everything else. If Max or I left one cup in the family room or forgot to return even one thing to our rooms, she flew off the handle.

Our house has always been like something out of *House Beautiful*, but Mom had really gone overboard about her rule of "a place for everything and everything in its place." If things weren't the way she thought they should be, she had a fit.

One night she came home late from her aerobics class, so Max and I made ourselves peanut butter and jelly sandwiches and plopped down in front of the television to eat. When we heard her come in, we called, "Hi, Mom," and kept on eating. Big mistake.

Mom went into the kitchen and saw the peanut butter, jelly, a few crumbs, a bag of potato chips, and the unwashed knife still on the counter.

"What will it take?" she shrieked.

Max and I looked at each other. Suddenly I wasn't mad at Max anymore. This was one of those times we had to stick together.

She was standing in the family room doorway with the peanut butter jar in one hand and the gooey jelly knife in the other.

"What will it take for you kids to learn to clean up after yourselves?"

"But Mom, we weren't finished," I began.

"Enough! Don't say another word! I work hard all day, slaving over people in their houses, stupid people who don't know what they want or how much they want to pay. I work hard for your father and for you two, cleaning this house and keeping things the way they should be. I try so hard to keep this family's reputation intact, and what do I get?" She paused, looking around. "Ingratitude! Sloppiness! I get *mess!*"

Max and I waited. We would have gone to the kitchen to clean up, but we didn't want to walk past Mom while she was armed with a jar of peanut butter.

"I just can't take this!" she yelled, then her chin began to quiver and her head lowered. "Get in there and clean up that mess," she said, her arm shaking as she pointed with the jelly knife. "And don't stop until everything is back *as it should be.*"

She turned on the heel of her leather aerobics shoe, and I heard her slam and lock the door of her bedroom. Max and I moved to the kitchen and began to clean up.

"What brought that on?" asked Max, wiping the counter. "Is she going through a mid-life crisis?"

"Where in the world did you hear about that?"

"I read it in *Newsweek*. There are hormonal and social changes in people's lives as they approach forty." I didn't know what to say, so Max kept on. "She's nearly forty, isn't she?"

I shrugged. "She's thirty-six, but I don't think she's going through any radical changes. She doesn't act any older than she used to."

I folded down the top of the potato chip bag. "But I do think there is something going on that she's not telling us."

"With Dad?"

"Yeah." I didn't know how much Max had noticed or heard around the house. "It's just a tough time. Things will be better when Dad's job settles down. I guess everyone is feeling the pressure."

Max stopped wiping and got that serious look that makes him look like a short, old man. "Do you think Mom and Dad love each other?"

I had never thought about it. "Sure, they do," I said with a shrug, wiping jelly goo off the edge of the jar. "All parents do, they just don't show it much after they've been married a long time."

"When is the last time you saw them kiss?"

"Honestly, Max, I don't know. I'm sure they kiss when they're alone."

"People on television kiss all the time. I see teenagers kissing in the mall all the time. I've seen Grandma and Grandpa kiss. But I haven't seen Mom and Dad kiss or hold hands or anything in a long time."

He was right, and as I bent to put the peanut butter in the pantry I wondered if he had a point. We're not a real affectionate family, but Mom and Dad did kiss us more than they kissed each other.

"Don't worry about it, Max." I smiled. "Mom and Dad can handle their own problems when they're alone. It's dumb to worry about whether they kiss or not."

I stood back and looked at the kitchen we had just cleaned. "There! Is everything back *as it should be?*" I asked, mimicking Mom's words.

"Fat chance," Max answered, going to his room.

5

The pressure of singing in front of people in the choir room was nothing to the silent pressure Max and I felt alone at home, so I stretched my hour-long, after-school rehearsals into an hour and a half by hanging around to talk and help Mr. Williams file music. We were required to stay three afternoons a week, but I volunteered to stay after every day. "Whatever I can do, Mr. Williams," I said. "I'll file music, sew costumes, sweep floors—you just name it."

"That's quite commendable, young lady," he said, but I caught him looking at me curiously. I knew it wasn't natural to want to stay after school every day, but I didn't mind, particularly when Andrea came up with her brilliant idea— we asked Mr. Williams if Andrea could join the production as my understudy. I couldn't believe Andrea wanted to be my shadow for a change!

I should have known she'd think of something like that because she wanted to be near Chip McKinnon so much, but I liked her company.

"She can help me study, and she can learn the part in case I get sick or something," I told Mr. Williams. "And she really is a good square dancer."

Mr. Williams asked Andrea to lead the other kids in some square-dance patterns, and she did a great job. Her dainty hands and feet, which had never done her any good at cheerleading tryouts, were designed to dance. As she whirled around on the choir room floor with her hair shining in the light, she looked like a humming-bird in flight. I had to admit she was a better dancer than I was, and Mr. Williams listed her in the production crew as "square-dance coordinator and understudy."

I knew Andrea's main reason for joining the production was to be near Chip McKinnon, but when I asked her about it, she looked surprised and said, "I just wanted to be with my best friend!"

She may have been my best friend, but she turned into Jell-O whenever Chip walked into the room. She'd gaze up at him with a you're-the-pepperoni-on-my-pizza look that made me want to gag.

Once we were all sitting around the choir room waiting for Mr. Williams to begin rehearsal. Chip was sitting nearby reading a library book, and we girls were talking about our favorite movie stars.

"I think Tom Cruise is the dreamiest," one girl said. "Don't you?"

I nodded, but Andrea raised her voice in Chip's direction and made a nauseating declaration: "Oh, I don't think Tom Cruise is so hot. I like guys who are tall, thin, blond, and blue-eyed. Find me a guy like *that,* and I'd follow him anywhere!"

Andrea was so obvious the other girls giggled, and I thought Chip suddenly looked uncomfortable, but he pretended not to hear. *Honestly, Andrea,* I thought to myself, *can't you be just a little more subtle?*

I wondered if she ever felt jealous of the time Chip and I spent practicing our duet. At first we simply stood behind the grand piano and sang the song. Even then, I was embarrassed because I always rested my hands on the top of the piano lid and once when we were done, my palm prints were left there because my hands had been sweating buckets. But after we learned the song, Mr. Williams wanted to stage it. He put us together so closely that I could see my reflection staring back from those blue eyes only five inches from mine.

"Why do they make up stories that link my name with yours?" Chip sang to me, and I had to answer, "Why do the neighbors gossip all day behind their doors?" At first I couldn't look at him without blushing. But after days and days of practice and hours and hours of gazing into those baby blues, I got used to it. In fact, one afternoon as Andrea and I walked home from school I confided a little secret to her.

"You know, Chip's really cute and all, but honestly, on some days he has the worst breath!"

"You're kidding." Andrea couldn't believe Chip had a single flaw.

"Maybe it was just something he ate, but I honestly thought I was going to faint today during practice. I think it was onions."

"Maybe it was garlic." Andrea giggled. "You know, they say if you eat enough garlic your skin will even begin to smell. The garlic smell will come out through your pores."

"That's repulsive." I kicked a pebble off the sidewalk. "But if that's true, Chip McKinnon must have eaten a barrel of onions today for lunch. He simply reeked!"

Andrea giggled, then threw her head back in a loud laugh. "Can you imagine?" she asked, batting her lashes coyly. "Can you imagine what the other girls would think if they knew gorgeous Chip McKinnon had bad breath? That their idol from afar reeks of onion?"

"Don't you dare say a word!" My cheeks flamed. "Chip would know who started that rumor because I'm his singing partner. Besides, he's really a nice guy, and I'd hate to hurt his feelings or have him get mad at me."

"Don't worry." Andrea smiled at me. "I promise. Chip's smelly secret is safe with me."

6

I couldn't believe it. Dad was actually home for dinner, and Mom had knocked herself out preparing it. She must have canceled her appointments for the day and spent most of the afternoon in the kitchen. There was a baking hen, with its roasted drumsticks in frilly paper, mashed potatoes, cranberry sauce, corn on the cob, sweet rolls, green beans, fruit salad, and even a chocolate pie.

"What happened?" asked Max when he came into the dining room. "Did I fall asleep for ten months? Is it Christmas already?"

"Shhhhh," I warned him. "Mom worked hard on this, so don't knock it."

It seemed so strange. For weeks we had eaten dinner quietly on the kitchen bar, just Max and I or just Mom and Max (if I was late from rehearsals), but it had been months since our whole family had been together in the dining room.

Max's eyes were shining and he couldn't wait to eat. Dad smiled, but he seemed tired, and Mom was unusually sparkly and cheerful. She had on a pretty new periwinkle blue sweat suit that matched her eyes, but something bothered me. Her smile had an edge on it, and I had seen that same edge when our neighbor accidentally drove through her prize rose bushes. "It's OK," she had told Mr. Bushnell, smiling that sharp smile. But she had come back into the house and burst into tears.

Dad smiled at Max and rumpled my hair as he sat down to eat. "How's my gypsy girl?" he asked. "I hear you've been busy in some sort of secret project at school."

"That's right, Dad." I smiled. "And you're going to get the surprise of your life."

"When is this surprise, or is that a secret, too?"

"It's in May. Just mark your calendar for May 12 and don't make any plans."

"You got it, gypsy gal."

Mom passed the corn, smiling at Dad. "Glen, dear, can you carve the hen, or shall I?"

Dad shrugged. "You're much better at it. Why don't you do the honors." He turned his attention to Max.

"Max, how would you like to go up to Huntsville with me this summer? I've got to go up there on business, and I thought you'd like to see the Huntsville NASA headquarters."

"Could I? That'd be great!" Max would drop even his most secret experiments for a chance to

50

go anywhere that had anything to do with the space program. Of course we lived near Kennedy Space Center, and Dad and Max had already visited Houston. This would be Max's first visit to Huntsville.

"Could we visit Miss Baker's grave?"

"Whose *what?*" asked Mom, making a sour face.

"Miss Baker," Max explained. "She was the squirrel monkey who flew into space in 1959. She's buried at the Alabama Space and Rocket Center on Tranquility Base."

Dad grinned. "Of course. We'll have plenty of time. My supervisors are trying to get me to take some time off because the pressure's been pretty intense lately."

He stirred his mashed potatoes into the gravy. "In fact, Son," he went on, looking down, "we could take the entire summer. We could spend a few weeks in Huntsville while I finish up a project there and then go up to Washington to see the National Air and Space Museum. You've always wanted to see the shuttle *Enterprise.*"

I thought Max would wet his pants. Not even a basket of Twinkies could get him this excited. He was so thrilled he couldn't feel the chill creeping over the dinner table.

I felt it. It came from Mom.

"And just when," she spoke, her words icily clear, "do you intend to live in this house again?"

Dad glanced at her and even I could read

51

the "not now" warning his eyes flashed. But Mom ignored it. "You grace us with your presence just this once, is that it? I know you've been spending a lot of time at work. I know everyone at the Space Center is a mess because of the tragedy, but I also know you've been avoiding us."

She was holding a butter knife, and the pat of butter she was about to spread on her bread was slowly slipping and sliding off the knife toward the linen tablecloth. It would make a stain and she would gripe plenty tomorrow, but now she didn't care. She sat there, glaring at Dad, and the hand that held the butter knife trembled slightly.

"Claire, we will discuss this later. Right now I'd like to enjoy this delicious meal and talk to my children."

Max and I looked at each other. Max had been caught by surprise, and his pitiful can't-we-get-out-of-here? expression made me want to cry. But I didn't feel any better, and I didn't see a way out.

"We can't ignore this any longer." Mom sat her knife down and folded her hands. "I want the children to hear this." She looked at me and Max, then she turned to Dad. "Glen, if you can't live with us, then I want you to live without us. If you can't be home with us and be there for us when we need you, I want you to move out. If you can't promise us that things will be different from tomorrow on, I want you to pack your bags tonight."

She seemed cool and calm, but her head jerked in a spasm of surprise when Dad folded his napkin and stood up. "I can't make that promise, Claire," he said simply. He walked to his room, and I heard the closet door slide open. He was packing.

Mom hesitated only a moment. "Cassie, Max," she commanded, picking up her own knife and fork, "eat your dinner."

The festive dinner seemed utterly tasteless now, and a lump kept rising in my throat that made it difficult to swallow. Max wasn't doing much better. At first I thought he'd cry, but he kept his fork going from plate to mouth in an automatic pattern. We both listened for noises from the back of the house where Dad was packing his suitcase.

When we heard the front door close, Max opened his mouth: "Mom—"

"Shut up." She was busy cutting and eating the now-cold chicken. How could she ignore Dad? He was leaving!

Max looked at me, bewildered.

I knew how to do it. "I'm finished; may I be excused." I said it as a statement, not a question, so Mom didn't have to answer. I slipped out of my seat and nodded at Max, who did the same.

We hurried to the living room and brushed aside the sheer curtain. We could see Dad loading a suitcase into the car. He locked the trunk, patted his pockets as if searching for something he'd forgotten, then he scanned the front of the house.

He saw us and smiled a weak little smile. He silently mouthed the words, "I'll be back soon," and waved. We smiled little fake smiles, too, and waved as if he were just going down to the corner grocery. Then he got into his car and pulled out of the driveway while we just stood there watching.

After a while Max spoke. "Do you think she knew he'd leave?"

"No," I said, "but I'm not surprised he did."

Max and I moved to the couch and sat down in silence. It was my night to clean the kitchen, but I didn't want to go back in there with Mom around. After a while I heard her push her chair back and leave the kitchen to go to their bedroom—her bedroom tonight. The lock clicked.

Max and I went in and cleaned the kitchen.

That night Mom stayed in her room, and I sat in Max's room watching him examine the gerbils. Max was pretending to be a vet tonight. He had added a stethoscope and a pocketful of pens to the old lab coat costume. Jessica was hyperactive; she wouldn't be still enough for Max to measure her.

"Here, Cassie," he motioned toward the cage, "if you can grab her by the tail and hold her upside down I can measure her with no problem."

54

"OK." I didn't really like messing around with rodents, but if Max could handle them, I knew I could. "Do I grab the end of the tail or the beginning of it?"

"The beginning."

As Max held the ruler against the squirming gerbil, he thought it was time to ask a question.

"Cassie?"

"Huh?"

"Why couldn't Dad promise Mom that things would be different?" Max whispered. "What things? Doesn't he care about us anymore?"

I shook my head. "I don't know what went wrong. I think he still cares, but maybe he just thinks it is wrong to promise something that is impossible." I put Jessica back into her cage. "Apparently he thinks it is better not to make a promise than to break it."

"Do you agree?"

"Sure."

"What about the promise you made never to hit me again?"

"Max, what are you talking about?"

"The time I broke your Chinese doll. You gave me a black eye, and Mom made you promise never to hit me again."

That Chinese doll—I had nearly forgotten. Dad had brought me a beautiful doll from China, a fragile doll meant to be displayed, not played with. I was nine and decided that I'd keep her in her perfectly beautiful condition until the day I died. But Max, who was about five, was fascinated by the doll and couldn't resist taking her off my dresser. He says he accidentally broke her arm, but when he looked into the gaping hole where her arm had been, he realized she was made of Chinese newspapers! So the five-year-old whiz kid *purposely* destroyed my doll, unraveling the tiny strips of newspaper that had been inside her arms, legs, and body. I don't know *what* he was doing— probably hoping he could learn a Chinese word or two.

I had gotten so mad that I belted him. Mom had gotten so mad that she made me promise never to hit my brother again. Of course, I didn't go around hitting Max all the time, but there had been a couple of times since then that we've given each other a good whack.

"You promised not to hit me again, and you've broken that promise."

"So what, Max? You've hit me, too!"

"All brothers and sisters fight."

"Well, I don't go around hitting you now."

"But, Cassie, the point is that you made a promise you couldn't keep. But it made Mom happy, didn't it? Why couldn't Dad make a promise just to keep Mom happy?"

I didn't have an answer. "Max, we were kids and they are grown-ups. There's a difference." I looked at poor Max who was desperately seeking a logical explanation. "I don't know what it is, Max, but there's a difference."

7

I was quiet for the next few days at school. I
didn't want to talk to anyone, even Andrea.
"What is wrong with you?" she kept asking me
one day at lunch until at last I muttered something about Mom being in a terrible mood since
Dad had gone on a business trip.

"He's gone and Mom's been a terror to live
with," I said with a shrug. "I just can't wait until
he gets back."

"When's that?"

"Oh, next week sometime. I forget," I hedged.
"He's been really busy."

"I know." Andrea dunked a long french fry
into a puddle of catsup. "My parents were saying
just the other day that they really miss getting
together with your folks to play cards. They used
to do that every weekend, remember? But they
haven't done that since—"

"Since the shuttle blew up," I finished. "Well, those days are gone, believe me." I let more slip out than I had intended to, but suddenly it felt good to tell someone the truth. "Andrea, I really don't know when my dad is coming back. My parents had a big fight, and they don't get along like they used to."

"Are you sure he's coming back?"

"Yes. He promised he would. But I don't know when."

"Wow, your parents." Andrea was looking at me with awe. "I never would have thought it would happen to your parents."

"What would happen?" I was growing impatient with her, best friend or not. I shrugged. "Nothing's happened."

"They could get a divorce, you know. It's no big deal. More than half of the kids in our class have divorced parents, and look at them—do you see any of them crying over their lunch trays?"

I glanced around. She was right. Everyone around me was laughing, talking, and eating like nothing in the world was wrong. Chip and his friends were in a corner talking about the movie they saw last weekend. "It was awesome," I heard one boy shout. "This submachine gun just blew the head off the creature, and green blood splashed all over the place!"

How disgusting. I looked back at Andrea and nodded. "It's nothing, I tell you," Andrea went on, trying to be helpful. "Some of the most popular kids in school live with their mothers, and they are perfectly OK. They don't have two strict parents like you and I do." She caught sight of Mandi McCormack, a cheerleader, and motioned for Mandi to come over.

"Andrea, what's up?" asked Mandi, a friend of Andrea's from cheerleading tryout days. I tried to shush Andrea, but it was too late. Mandi was in our math class and seemed friendly, but I didn't want the entire school to know about my personal life.

"Tell Cassie what it's like when parents get a divorce."

Mandi glanced at me, then smiled. "It's rough at first," she said, flipping her bangs out of her eyes, "then it gets better. But it's a pain when your mom is dating and there are strange men at the house all the time. You never know when your mom's going to walk in with some guy and find you on the couch in your nightgown."

Her eyes narrowed. "But the worst part is when your mother remarries and you get a step-father. I've hated all five of mine, and if you get one, you'll probably hate him, too. They either want to be your dad or your buddy or your boy-friend, or they just ignore you like you don't even live there. Take my advice—if your mom looks like she's going to get married again, call your dad and ask to live with him for a change. Unless he's remarried, too—then you'll just have to wait for one of them to divorce again."

I gulped and whispered, "Thanks for the advice."

"Hey, no problem." Mandi breezed over toward her cheerleader friends, the noise of her gum cracking through the crowd, but her words echoed in my head: *You'll just have to wait for one of them to divorce again.* Divorce *again?*

Andrea looked at me, grinning. "I told you, it's a piece of cake. Whatever happens, you'll be fine."

"How can you say that?" I whispered, keeping my voice down so no one else would hear. "Mandi may be popular and all, but my dad always says that hate will eat you up. She sounds like she hates the whole world."

Andrea shrugged. "Hey, I'm no psychologist. But she looks like she's doing fine to me."

I watched where Mandi stood talking with some friends. Scott Iverson, a basketball player, walked by, and Mandi gave him a coy once-over with her eyes and smiled. Scott stopped and grinned back at her, running his hand up and down her back.

"When did Mandi start going out with Scott Iverson?" I asked. "Doesn't he have a sort of wild reputation?"

Andrea raised her eyebrows and looked over to where they stood. "I didn't think she was going out with Scott. Last week she was going out with Tim Richards."

"I've heard he's no saint, either."

"It's Mandi's own business," Andrea said

finally. "If she dates wild guys, I'm sure she can handle herself."

"My folks won't let me date until I'm sixteen," I mumbled. "At least that's what they say now. If they get divorced, who knows what they'll be doing?" I looked down at my lunch, which looked about as appetizing as sawdust.

"Nothing is going to happen," Andrea said firmly. "Your mom and dad just had a fight, and your dad will be home soon. I'm sure of it."

Andrea was right. It simply had to be. There's no way I could ever be like Mandi. We're just too different.

For the next two weeks I waited for Dad to come home. I knew it could be at any time, on any day. Every time I heard a car pull into the driveway at night I ran to my window, but it was always either a car just turning around or one of Mom's decorating clients. Dad didn't call, write, or show up. I was beginning to wonder if we would ever see him again.

I thought about sneaking out of class one day and calling him at work, but a systems analyst at NASA can be hard to find. He could be working anywhere. I'd have to leave a message and go to class, and then he'd have to return my call at home where Mom might answer. I didn't want to make him talk to Mom until he was ready.

So I tried to put Dad out of my mind and concentrate on schoolwork and *Oklahoma!* Andrea's interest in the musical had been fading since I told her Chip had bad breath, so she only stayed for the three required rehearsals while I still stayed at school every day until nearly four-thirty. But there was an interesting new development: Chip began to stay after school with me!

I can honestly say that I never did anything to lead him on, but we spent so much time practicing together that I suppose it was normal for us to begin to talk about other things. He has a champion keeshond puppy named Macbeth, and I told him about Suki. Suki was too old to be show quality, I laughed, but she was the best dog I'd ever seen, and her ancestors had been champion show dogs.

"But I've never really been interested in dog shows," I confessed. "I just like my dog for a pet."

"Now that's where you're missing something," said Chip, and he told me that a trained dog is a better pet and a more valuable dog. "Why don't you meet me at the city stadium on Sunday afternoon? There's an American Kennel Club dog show, and I'm entering Macbeth."

So we had a date. And Chip walked me home from school, and we talked about dogs, and school, and the musical all the way to my house. And never once did I think about Mom or Dad or anything depressing. Not once.

8

All day Saturday I could think of nothing but Chip and the dog show. When I asked Mom if she'd mind dropping me off on Sunday, she had only one absent-minded comment: "Two o'clock? Sure, dear, just write it on the calendar." And wonder of wonders, Max didn't even ask to go along.

On Saturday afternoon Max, Suki, and I settled in front of the television for the afternoon "creature feature" as Mom left for her weekly tennis lesson. She paused before going out the door, her keys jangling against the knob.

"Cassie?"

"What, Mom?"

She bit her lip. "If your father calls—" She shook her head. "Never mind."

The creature had just climbed out of the murky swamp to attack the unsuspecting lovers in the convertible when the phone rang. Max looked at me. "Do you think it's Dad?"

I didn't wait around to guess. It could be Chip, so I flew to the kitchen phone.

"Hello?"

"Hello, gypsy girl. How are you and the whiz kid doing?"

"We're fine, Dad. How are you?" Max ran to get on the extension phone while I talked. It was really good to hear from him.

"Where are you?"

"I took an apartment on Cocoa Beach. You'll love it. I can hear the beach when I go to sleep and first thing when I wake up every morning. It's close to everything and, of course, it's only temporary."

"Temporary? Then you are coming home!"

Dad was silent for a moment. "Actually, honey, it's temporary until I can buy a condo. Your mother and I haven't settled things yet, but I'm sure I won't be coming back home to live. I'll come by to get you and Max, though, and we'll do things just like we used to. And Max, are you there?"

"Right here, Dad," said Max on the extension phone.

"I'm still planning that trip to Huntsville, and I want you to come. Cassie, you're welcome to come, too, but I think you'll be bored."

"That's OK, Dad. I'd rather stay here this summer."

"Anyway, I called to let you kids know I'll be

over later to pick you up. You can spend the night with me tonight, and tomorrow I want to take you both sailing. We'll spend the whole day on the water."

I felt . . . no, I *heard* my heart sink. I felt sick. "But Dad, I'm going to a dog show tomorrow. It's kind of a special thing for me."

"A dog show? You'd rather go to a dog show? OK, I'll take you guys to the dog show. We can go sailing next weekend."

"No, Dad, you don't understand. I'm meeting a friend from school at the dog show." Honestly, parents can be so dense sometimes! Did I have to spell it out?

"You're meeting a friend?"

"She's got a boyfriend, Dad," interrupted Max.

"Ah, now I understand. A boyfriend. You'd rather go to the dog show with a boyfriend than sailing with your own father who you haven't seen in two weeks."

Why was he laying a guilt trip on me? Was I the one who walked out? Was it my fault I hadn't seen him in two weeks? I've never been angry at my father, but at that moment I could have slammed the phone down with pleasure.

But I took a deep breath and tried to be calm. "Mom's already agreed to take me to the dog show, and I already promised Chip I'd meet him there. I'm sorry, Dad, but I made these plans first."

Dad was silent for a moment, then his voice was clipped: "Forget it." We wouldn't be seeing him this weekend at all. Dad was obviously angry with me, and I felt guilty for ruining the weekend for Max, too.

"OK, Cassie, that's fine," he went on. "I'll give you guys a call next weekend, and we'll work out something then. But mark your calendars because I'm your father and I expect to see you on weekends. Tell your mother—"

"Tell her what?"

"Tell her I'll be over Wednesday morning to talk to her. And tell her that I'll be picking you two up every Saturday morning beginning next week. 'Bye."

The phone line clicked, and I felt angry and confused at the same time. Guilty, too, because I had been missing Dad and hoping to see him, but when it came down to choosing between Chip and Dad, I'd chosen Chip. It wasn't fair. Why should I *have* to choose?

Max came into the kitchen and reached into the refrigerator for an apple. "Did he really mean that every Saturday we'll be staying on Cocoa Beach?"

"I don't know." I thought about all the Saturdays that stretched ahead of me. I was growing up, I wanted to be with my friends, and weekends were our only free time. Did this mean I wouldn't be able to stay over at Andrea's or meet Chip on Saturdays or do *anything* for the rest of my life?

I dialed Andrea's number.

"Hello?" It was Andrea. I was glad she answered instead of her mother.

"My life is ending," I said, my voice catching.

"What? Cassie? What are you talking about?"

"My dad is moving into a condo on the beach, and he wants me to spend every Saturday and Sunday with him for the rest of my life."

"That's crazy. No one could want you around that much," she teased.

"Andrea, I'm serious! What am I going to do? What if there is a weekend when I don't want to come? I can't tell him that—it would hurt his feelings! What if I wanted to spend the weekend with you or something?"

"I see your problem."

"It has already been a problem. This weekend Dad wanted to have us over and I told him no. He was mad, I could tell."

"Why didn't you want to go this weekend?"

I decided to confide the news of the century to Andrea. "Are you ready for this? I'm meeting Chip tomorrow at the dog show!"

Andrea laughed loud and long, then she grew quiet. "You're not kidding? You're really meeting Chip? He *asked* you to meet him?"

"Yeah, alert the media." I giggled. Boy, it felt good to tell somebody who would appreciate the news! Then I took a deep breath and kept my voice calm. "He asked me to meet him, and my mom said she'd drop me off. It should be fun."

"Oh, stop pretending to be so cool," Andrea

chided. "I know you're excited. But I can't believe that out of all the girls in school, Chip McKinnon asked you to meet him."

It wasn't hard to hear the sarcasm in her words. "What do you mean?" I asked. "Why shouldn't he ask me? We've become good friends, and I like him a lot. I think he likes me, too."

"That's what I can't believe."

"Andrea Milford, how can you say that? You're supposed to be my best friend!"

"Come on, Cassie. Mandi has been trying to get him to notice her for months, and you know how gorgeous she is!"

"Yeah, well, maybe she's not his type."

"And you are? Come on, get real!"

"All right, I will. Good-bye, Andrea."

I hung up and sat by the kitchen bar trembling in fury. She was just jealous, I knew, because *she* was the one who had been trying for months to get Chip to notice her. But Chip didn't know me as Andrea's shadow or "ordinary Cassie." Chip knew me as a smiling, scarlet dancer! Someone special! We sang to each other and worked hard together, and something clicked! Andrea would never understand.

"Come on, get real." Her words echoed in my head. I would! Andrea would see! I ran into my room and stood in front of the mirror. It took a minute for the truth to sink in, but there it was. I wasn't anything to be ashamed of, but my mirror told the truth—there was no beautiful scarlet dancer reflected there. In my dreams, maybe, but in reality, no.

I threw myself over my bed and let the tears come. Why should Chip look at me? I could sing, sure, but what good was that? We'd have one date, and he'd know I was more stupid than my kid brother, less polished than my mother, and permanently unavailable on weekends. I was a thirteen-year-old mess, and from this point on, nothing in my life was going to go right.

9

It was a beautiful Sunday afternoon that promised to be hot and bright. Suki and I looked our best. I debated for hours over what to wear, finally deciding on a denim skirt and a bright yellow sleeveless blouse that would show off my tan.

Mom raised her eyebrows when I snapped Suki's leash on her collar. "You're taking that old dog?" she asked. "Are you sure she can walk that far in this heat without collapsing?"

"I'll take care of her, Mom. I just thought she might enjoy seeing some other dogs."

Mom shook her head, but the truth was, I wanted to take Suki mainly to have something to do with my hands. I mean, what do you do walking around a dog show unless you're walking a dog? And suppose Chip didn't show up? I'd be wandering around all alone. So I decided

71

Suki could go too. I was nervous and needed her unwavering support.

Mom let us out at the corner of the city stadium, and we walked through the gates onto the baseball field where several bright blue tents had been set up. There was no sign of Chip, but I breathed a sigh of relief. He didn't have to meet my mother, so he wouldn't be so impressed with her that I seemed dowdy by comparison.

Suki and I blended into the flow of people and their dogs. Several tents sheltered rings where dogs were being judged with their owners. Other tents offered information, refreshments, and a place to sit.

Chip had promised to meet me by the refreshment stand at two o'clock. I waited until one minute after two before heading in that direction because I didn't want to seem too eager. Thankfully, he was there.

"Hi." He had been looking for me in the other direction and my voice surprised him.

"Hi, Cassie. Is this your dog?" he asked as he stooped down and scratched Suki's head.

"Yes. I know it's silly to bring her along if she's not in the show, but I just thought it would be fun. I mean, there just aren't many places a dog can go."

"I think it's great. My parents are grooming Macbeth—the keeshond judging begins in half an hour. Come on, I'd like you to meet my folks."

I hadn't counted on meeting Chip's parents,

but they put me right at ease. Mr. McKinnon was tall and quiet, with golden hair just like Chip's. Mrs. McKinnon was the noisier of the two and shorter than I was.

"It's always nice to meet a friend of Chip's," said Mr. McKinnon, shaking my hand.

"Why Chip, she's a real sugah bear," exclaimed his mother in a drawl that made me smile. She smiled right back at me and asked, "Where are you from, honey?"

Like most people, she was surprised to hear that I'm a native Floridian. Nearly everyone in our county moved here from somewhere else. My guess was that Mrs. McKinnon was from the deep South somewhere—maybe up north in South Carolina or Georgia.

"Well, we're real excited that you can join us today. We're thrilled that Chip is finally getting to show Macbayeth."

Macbeth was a sight. I had heard of keeshond dogs, but I had never seen one. Macbeth was nothing but a mass of fluff with four paws, a mane of soft fur, and two button brown eyes that blinked occasionally. He looked more like a toy lion than a dog.

Chip's parents were a real team. His mother was clipping the dog's toenails from one side while Chip's dad brushed Macbeth's fur from another. Chip was busy untangling a knot in the dog's lead. Much more slender than the bulky leash Suki was wearing, the lead was a combination collar/leash that would help Chip control Macbeth in the ring.

All around us, dogs and owners were grooming and clipping. One large poodle was having his hair fluffed and sprayed by an anxious owner. Another dog sat calmly while his owner applied clear nail polish to his toenails. I was amazed. Suki would go nuts if I came near her with a can of hair spray.

"He's done, Son. He's all yours." Mr. McKinnon stepped back, and Macbeth looked up at Chip. Now there was a case of dog/master love if I ever saw one. Macbeth stood expectantly, jumped down from his grooming box, and together he and Chip and Suki and I walked toward a ring where three judges stood holding clipboards.

There were only two keeshond dogs entered in the show, and Macbeth easily won "best of breed." Chip was thrilled. He had done a great job, running in a deliberate circle in the ring with Macbeth by his side, and I had learned a lot. "If you were four years younger," I whispered to Suki, "I'd have you in a ring, too."

After Chip had collected the blue ribbon, we joined his parents and the dogs at a table under the refreshment tent. At four o'clock, Macbeth would compete with the other "best of breed" winners for "best of show." I would have been scared stiff, knowing I had to perform again, but the McKinnons were all relaxed. Mr. McKinnon brought us each a Coke, and we sat and watched the other dogs and their owners walk by.

"Have you ever noticed how much owners and their dogs resemble one another?" asked Mr. McKinnon.

We laughed. "It's true," agreed Mrs. McKinnon, smiling. "Look over they-ah." She discreetly pointed toward a large Afghan hound and its owner. The owner, a tall woman with a long face, did look amazingly like her tall, long-faced dog.

"Check this out over here," Chip said. He rolled his eyes toward a heavy gentleman strolling with his bulldog. Both dog and master were stout. Both had paunchy cheeks and button brown eyes.

"Well, Chip, how does that apply to you?" I teased.

Mr. McKinnon laughed. "She's got you there, Son." He smiled as he slipped his arm comfortably around his wife. "But you haven't seen everything, Cassie. When he wakes up in the morning with his hair standing up all around his head, he and Macbeth could pass for brothers."

Chip took the good-natured ribbing with a smile. "Sure, Dad," he said, reaching over to take my hand. "But let's spare her the gruesome details, OK? I'd like to keep her around a while."

(If touching the face of God is anything like the feeling of Chip's hand around mine, it must be incredibly awesome.)

Macbeth didn't win best of show, but at that point, I was past caring. It was still a perfect day.

10

Monday morning was something else. Andrea snubbed me in the hall and didn't even look my way in English class. *She's still mad about Chip,* I thought, *but there's nothing I can do about that.*

But I tried. After English I stopped her in the hall. "Andrea, I want to talk to you."

"Oh, Cassie, it's you." Her sarcastic words clipped through the bustle around us. "How was your date with Chip?"

"It was fine. Actually," I couldn't stop a smile, "it was great."

"I'd love to hear all about it, but I really can't stop to talk now."

"Andrea, don't be silly. Don't be mad at me."

She tossed her blonde mane and pretended to examine her manicured fingernails. "Me? Mad at you? Don't be stupid. I wouldn't waste my energy." She looked up at me and raised her eyebrows quizzically. "I'm not mad, I'm just amazed."

"Amazed?"

"Amazed that Chip McKinnon would agree to meet you anywhere. But don't you think it's funny that he took you to a dog show? Were *you* the one he entered?"

That sorry joke struck Andrea as terribly funny, and she turned sharply and walked down the hall laughing, *yuk, yuk, yuk*.

By second period everyone was laughing. "Hey, Jones, did you hear about Chip taking Cassie Perkins to the dog show? He entered her and she won first place!" *Har, har, har.*

After third period a wimpy sixth grader came up and stared at me.

"What do you want?" I asked.

"Nothing." He grinned. "Woof, woof, woof!"

My only consolation came at fourth period when I passed Chip in the hall. I thought he'd be so embarrassed that he'd ignore me, but he stopped for a minute.

"Hey, Cassie, I'm sorry about all the junk going around," he said, his cheeks red.

"It's OK." I smiled, grateful to know he wasn't so embarrassed he'd never speak to me again. "It'll blow over."

I really thought nothing could be worse than that dumb joke, but I had underestimated Andrea. Just before my last class, a new disaster literally came my way.

I was sitting in history when I saw a note being passed from the third row of desks over to the fourth, my row. I was impressed. Whatever this note was, it had started in the back of the classroom near Andrea's desk, gone up the first row, down the second, up the third, and now was going to come my direction. It must be major gossip.

The girl in front of me read it and hesitated to hand it back, but I had seen it coming, and I held my hand out when the teacher turned to write on the board. "I don't know who it's from," she whispered.

The note was simple and cruel:

Question: What sings like a bird, dances like a monkey, and smells worse than a barrel of onions?
Answer: Chip McKinnon. Ask his singing partner, Cassie Perkins! Pass it on!

I felt my stomach turn over. I wanted to throw up. I stuffed the note into my history book just as the bell rang, and I turned to look across the room at Andrea. She looked back at me, tossed her head, and left.

Had Chip heard? Whether he had read the note or not, someone would be sure to pass the news on to him, I knew. Worse yet, the joke had the ring of truth—Chip did sing, he wasn't the best dancer, and he *had* smelled of onions several times, and I was the one who had told Andrea about it! I was probably the only one close enough to smell it! I was guilty, guilty, guilty.

For the first time I was afraid to go to choir rehearsal. Today was an important rehearsal, too, because we were going to be measured for costumes. But how could I ever face Chip? He'd know I was guilty from the look on my face!

I chickened out and went home like a coward. I'd just face Mr. Williams tomorrow and tell him, quite truthfully, that I felt sick at my stomach. But I couldn't face Chip today, and probably never again.

I hadn't been home at three o'clock in weeks, and the house was still. Max was home—I had seen his bicycle in the garage—but he was probably locked in his room working on an experiment or on his computer. Mom was gone, either to a client's house or to her spa, and there was a note on the refrigerator: "Be back at 5:30."

I fixed myself a Coke thinking maybe the bubbles or caffeine would help me feel better. Nothing could make me feel worse. The phone rang.

"Hello?"

"Hello, is Mrs. Perkins in?"

"No, may I take a message?"

"This is the secretary at Mr. Clarence's law office. We want to remind her of her appointment with us on Tuesday morning at nine o'clock."

"Tomorrow?"

"Yes, tomorrow morning."

"Thank you. I'll tell her."

So, Mom had a lawyer! Dad probably had one, too. That was why he wanted to meet with her Wednesday morning while Max and I were at school. What would they say to each other, I wondered. How do you tie up the loose ends of a marriage?

Max came into the kitchen. He was wearing his safari outfit, a khaki shirt with about twenty pockets, tan shorts, and a bush helmet. A gerbil stuck its head out of one pocket and wiggled his whiskers in my direction. "It's just Cassie," Max told the gerbil. He looked at me. "What are you doing home?"

"Sick. I've had the worst day of my entire life, and I'm sick to death of Andrea Milford."

Max whistled. "It must have been some fight. I thought you two were tight."

"We were. But ever since Chip McKinnon and I have been friends, Andrea's been public enemy number one."

I took a sip of my drink and watched Max. "Been on safari near the drainage ditch again, Max? Catch anything?"

"No." Max shrugged. "Last week we found a garter snake, a *Thamnophis sirtalis,* but I was hoping for something more exotic."

"Just don't bring home anything that slithers," I warned. "Mom will throw a fit."

Poor kid, we had a big problem that he didn't

even know about. "Sit down, Max. I think we should talk." I pulled out a barstool and looked across the counter. "Is there anything to eat around here?"

Max reached into a cupboard and pulled out a container filled with cookies. They smelled of peanut butter, but they were burned on the bottom.

"Mom made cookies?" I couldn't believe it. "When did she get in the mood to bake cookies?"

"She didn't. I made them." He pushed the container in my direction. "And I learned never to put a pan of cookies on the bottom of the oven."

I laughed and took a bite. "Pretty good, even if they are burned. I'll just eat the top part. Now sit down."

Max sat down at the bar and offered a piece of cookie to his gerbil. I had to tell him.

"Max, I think Mom and Dad are filing for divorce. A lawyer called. Mom's meeting him tomorrow."

"Maybe she's writing a new will or something."

"No, I don't think so. It's divorce, I'm sure."

I was surprised because Max didn't seem to care about my news one way or the other. He just kept feeding that gerbil that blasted cookie, and finally he looked up.

"Dad will be home soon, you'll see."

"No, Max, I don't think Dad will be home."

"You're wrong." Max stood up so quickly that his stool fell backwards to the floor. "Anyway, you've got something much more important to worry about now."

"What?"

"You just ate a peanut butter and algae cookie."

Even though Max couldn't admit it, I knew the *D* word was going to be a part of our lives forever. Divorce. The word sent chills down my spine. What would it mean? Would we have to move out of our house? Could Mom afford house payments on her salary? I knew she worked, but I honestly didn't know how much money she made. Dad had always acted as though her interior design work was basically a hobby. Could she support us?

What about Dad? Would we have to go live with him? If we did, would we ever see him? He worked all the time! Where would we go to school? Would I lose all my friends? Would I ever see Chip again? What if my dad's apartment had rules against dogs? I couldn't leave Suki behind!

I don't think I slept much that night, and even though I didn't feel like going to school the next day, I got up and dressed from habit. I was in a daze or something, and I passed Andrea in the hall without even seeing her, which was probably for the best. She was so stunned that I wasn't mad or hateful that she followed me into the girls' rest room out of sheer curiosity.

"What's wrong with you?"

I looked at her, and all of her nasty jokes came flooding back to me, even though they seemed like nothing compared to what was happening at home.

"After yesterday and all you did, how can you ask what's wrong?"

"Oh that." She shrugged. "I was mean, I know, and I'm sorry. After I got home I began to feel bad about what I did. I realized how upset you were when you didn't show up for rehearsal." She paused. "I'll tell Chip I made the whole thing up if it will make you feel better."

"That's OK, forget it. That's the least of my problems now."

Andrea gave me a closer look. "What else is wrong?" She rapped on my forehead with her knuckles and clicked her tongue to make a knocking sound. "Is there anyone at home in there?"

I sighed and dug in my purse for my hairbrush. "I may as well tell you. Mom and Dad are getting a divorce, I'm sure. I'm so confused I don't know what to feel."

"Why are they splitting?"

"Who knows?" Goodness, nothing in my life was going right, not even my hair. Brushing only made it frizzier. "I don't think my parents know why they're splitting. But neither one of them is talking to me about it, so I will probably never know. They probably think they're sparing me."

"That's awful, Cassie." She meant it.

"Yeah." I put my brush away and looked down at my books. I hadn't opened them outside class in two weeks. After my next report card I'd be grounded for life. "Well, what can I do? Nothing but hope they don't totally ruin my life."

"Good luck. You'll need it."

Some comfort you are, I thought. But I had a feeling she was right.

11

I saw how right Andrea was on Wednesday night. After dinner Mom told us to finish our homework quickly because Dad was coming over. This was it—the Big Explanation. I stuck my head in Max's room: "I told you so."

Max just stood there, his brown eyes filled with tears, and I was sorry I had said it. We both are close to Dad, but Max and Dad are superclose. When they used to work together on the computer in the family room, they looked more like brothers than father and son.

I sat down on Max's bed and tugged on his shirt. He wasn't in costume today. He was just an ordinary, confused kid. "It'll be OK," I whispered. "I promise."

"You should never make a promise you can't keep," Max mumbled. "That's what you always say."

"I'll keep this one, Max. I know we'll be OK."

The doorbell rang and we both jumped up. It was funny to think of Dad ringing the doorbell when he owned the place. We heard Mom greeting him politely, and Max's eyes squinched up like he was going to cry, big time. It was all so wrong.

"Max, don't do it," I commanded. "You can handle this. This is your mission. A scientist must be tough. A scientist must face pressure. You can do this." I grabbed his officer's cap from off his dresser and put it on his head. "Attention, General Max. The troops await your inspection."

Max lifted his chin, squared his shoulders, and nodded stiffly. We walked out together to face the test.

Dad decided to take us out for dessert to give us "the big talk." Actually, I think it was pretty low of Dad to do that. He must have figured that in a public place we'd be too embarrassed to make a scene. At the time, though, we had a faint hope it would be like old times again, with all four of us crowded into a booth at the ice cream parlor, girls on one side, guys on the other. Then Dad opened his mouth and began to talk.

He and Mom were getting a divorce, Dad explained. Of course, that didn't mean he didn't love us anymore. He just didn't love Mom like a husband should. But we would spend weekends with him, and several weeks each summer, and he would be sending money to Mom so she could keep the house and keep us in our school. "We don't want to upset your lives, too." He smiled a plastic smile.

He didn't want to upset us? I couldn't believe he could sit there, smiling, and say that. "Why are you getting a divorce?" I asked. I had to know.

"Honey, you just wouldn't understand." It was Mom's turn to smile. "We just think it is important for you to know we both still love you two very much."

"And Max, you mark your calendar for our summer trip," said Dad, slapping Max's leg playfully. "We're going to go to Huntsville, Washington, and even Houston if you want to. Whatever you want, Son, that's what we'll do. We'll have a great time."

Max turned his brown eyes on Dad and the dam burst, public place or not. He leaned against Dad, sobbing, and he didn't look like General Max anymore. He looked like a nine-year-old kid who has found himself in big, big trouble. I could barely make out his words: "Dad . . . Mom . . . I'm so sorry. I'll try to be better—honestly, I'll try to fix it. Whatever I did, I'm sorry! Please, Dad, come home, and I promise I'll be better!"

Dad looked at Mom, then he put his arms around Max.

"Max, I'm so sorry. I didn't know you felt this way. You didn't do anything. The divorce is not your fault. It's not Cassie's fault. You two didn't do anything! It just happened."

"It happened after the shuttle blew up, didn't it, Dad?" Max was still crying. "But they'll fix it, won't they? Then will you come back?"

Mom shook her head in disbelief, and Dad tried to explain. "Max, my job, NASA—none of those things has anything to do with it. Your mom and I just stopped loving each other the way we should."

I had heard all the smooth explanations I could take. "I know why you're getting a divorce," I whispered fiercely, my fists clenching tightly under the table. "You promised to love each other and you broke your promise! You quit trying. You both are always telling Max and me to keep going and never give up if we really believe in something. Why did you give up? Don't you believe in this family anymore?"

They both sat there quietly, Dad looking out the window and Mom studying her napkin. The waitress, a jolly lady with a smile as bright as her red hair, came over and plunked down the check.

"There now, was everything all right?" she chirped.

"Fine," said Dad. "Everything *was* just fine."

12

For days there was a huge ball of anger inside me, too big to be defined and too bitter to go away. Mom and I fought over everything from my clothes to my grades, which were lousy.

One night she found two of my history tests in the garbage can. A big, red *F* glared on each one. "Cassie, how can you be making *F*s when you practically live at that school?" she demanded. "What are you doing with your time? You're not studying, that's obvious."

I still didn't want to tell her about the production. If she found out about Chip, and the music, and the dancing, and the fun—I couldn't bear to have her take it away from me. The scarlet dancer . . . please, please, don't kill the scarlet dancer.

"I'll study harder." I gulped. "I'll spend more time in the library. It's Mrs. Hamilton, Mom—

she gives the trickiest tests. Even the smartest kids flunk her tests."

It wasn't exactly true, but Mom calmed down. "Bring me your next test paper," she said, turning to leave. "I expect to see an improvement."

Dad usually handled things like bad grades (of course, I was the only one who ever got them), and he usually just rumpled my hair and promised that Max would tutor me. But he wasn't around, and Mom didn't know how to handle his jobs at all.

Max and I had just managed to work up a passable excitement about the idea of sailing with Dad on our first weekend together when he called and canceled. He said he had to work, and that was fine with us. I just couldn't see myself out there on a boat trying my hardest to act like I was having a good time.

For a few days after that Max was unusually quiet and went to bed early. At school, Andrea stayed a safe distance away. We still ate lunch together and sat by each other in our classes, but we didn't talk about anything honest. It wasn't like we were best friends anymore. Sometimes I felt like we had just met and were trying to make up stupid conversations about the weather.

Andrea just didn't know what I was going through, and I think it made her uncomfortable to be around me. That was fine with me. Finally one day I took my lunch tray to the table where Mandi was sitting with one of her friends.

"Is this seat taken?" I asked.

Mandi looked up in surprise. "Well, no," she said with a smile. "Join us."

I sat down and lifted the bun off my hamburger. The hamburger patty was gray, and I couldn't help making a face.

"Just drown it in catsup and you won't think about how awful it looks," Mandi said, smiling. She looked over at me and raised an eyebrow. We weren't friends, exactly, and I knew she was curious about why I chose to sit with her instead of Andrea.

"What's up?"

"My mom and dad are getting a divorce." I said it casually as I struggled to open my stubborn milk carton. "Dad took us out last week, we sat down, Mom and Dad told us they were getting a divorce, they said they loved us, and that was that." I looked up at her. "So what happens now?"

Mandi's eyes were wide with surprise. "You mean they sat you down and talked to you? Honestly, that's the wildest thing I ever heard. My mother never once sat me down and told me anything. Usually I just hear dishes breaking or I wake up and my mother's husband is gone. The latest—" she stopped to bite the end of a dangling french fry, "left last night." She swallowed. "I came into the kitchen this morning and my mom gave me her it's-just-you-and-me-again speech."

She stopped to count on her fingers. "It's happened to me five times now. I guess I'm used to it."

Her words didn't make me feel any better, and she realized it. "Hey, come on." She leaned on her elbow and pulled on her oversized earring. "You'll make it. You've just got to learn to depend on yourself. No one else will ever care enough to stick around."

Carley, Mandi's friend, spoke up. "I knew my parents were finished the night my dad got drunk and Mom called the police on him." She shrugged. "The police car came with its siren going and all the neighbors stood outside to watch my parents duke it out. Dad punched Mom and a policeman had to hold him down, but then Mom kicked the cop. They both spent the night in jail, and my brother and I were put into foster care."

I wanted to throw up. I never knew such things went on with kids in my own school.

"I live with my mom and her boyfriend now," said Carley. "But I'm moving out the day I turn sixteen. Mandi's right. No one cares about me anymore, so I'm going to take care of myself."

I was relieved when lunch was over. I felt bad enough, but I knew what I was going through wasn't the worst that could happen to me. It was worse than anything Andrea or Chip could imagine, though, and I thought about hanging out with Mandi and Carley more often. They'd let me, I knew, but I honestly didn't think I belonged with them. They didn't care about anything but getting away from home as soon as they could. They seemed so angry; maybe Dad was right about anger eating a person up inside.

But I had something else inside me. I had an ambition. I had the heart of a smiling, scarlet dancer. I wanted to go places and sing. And if I had to, I'd do it by myself.

I felt totally alone. Since that awful day Andrea had played her little joke, Chip hadn't been around much. I still saw him at rehearsals, of course, but we sang our parts and went our own ways. I was still too embarrassed to look him in the eye.

But for that hour when those of us in the production cast were together, there was an electricity in the air that made me forget all about the divorce. There were only four weeks until our performance, and we knew our words, our music, and our gestures. All that remained was putting the pieces together.

Mr. Williams was a perfectionist. "We're only giving one performance," he told us sternly, "and we're going to do our absolute best. We're going to rehearse as if there were 5,000 people in the audience, and we're going to work and work until we could do this in our sleep."

Someone snickered, and Mr. Williams cast his eagle eye into our group. "Don't laugh," he cautioned. "Because even though you think you know your part, what can go wrong *will* go wrong during a performance, and if we haven't fixed all that can go wrong, we might as well resign ourselves to doing a sloppy job. And that, ladies and gentlemen, is something I will never do."

After hearing Mr. Williams give one of his speeches, I always wanted to stand up and give all I had. I would sing my best, dance my best, and submerge everything I had—including my problems—in the part of Laurie.

Fortunately, everyone else felt the same charge in the air. We pulled together as a team, and we had spent so much time together we really were a sort of family. So we worked, and sang, and analyzed, and offered ideas. This performance would be something the school would never forget.

After one run-through of the final song, Mr. Williams stood and applauded us. "That was great." He smiled. "We're almost ready for Broadway." He planned four dress rehearsals, one each week until the performance. Our costumes were bulky, and we girls weren't used to moving around in long skirts with layers of petticoats. Square dancing in all those skirts wasn't as easy as it looked.

Mr. Williams rehearsed the square dancing scene while we singers watched. Andrea and a long-legged basketball player named Eric Smith were the featured dancers, and she was sweating in her long skirts. Eric was working hard, too, but the guys wore jeans and western-style shirts, so they didn't battle the heat nearly as much as we girls did.

"I can't believe this is only April," Andrea moaned as she sank into a chair and fanned herself with her notebook. "Why, oh *why* did my parents choose to settle in Florida?"

"Stop complaining and be thankful for air-conditioning." I smiled at her. "My mom's been so tight with the budget she won't let us run our air conditioner until June. Max and I swelter every time we go into the house."

Money had been tight, and I had a hard time convincing Mother I needed thirty dollars for a special school activity. The money was for my costume, of course, which was sewn by students in the Home Ec department, but I still had to pay for the material. And I still wanted Mom and Dad to be surprised by the musical. They knew I was in a school "play or something," but they would never dream I was the lead singer. They had no idea the scarlet dancer existed.

Even though they wouldn't be coming together, I still wanted them to come more than anything in the world. This dream was the most important thing in the world to me, and when I was singing I could forget they weren't living together. Maybe I could even get them to sit together, and then maybe they'd be so caught up in the spirit of my success, they'd work out their problems. Maybe the scarlet dancer would make everything all right again.

Mr. Williams called for the singers, and Chip and I took our places to sing "People Will Say We're in Love." It was the first time we had done it since that horrible rumor, and it was pretty embarrassing. "Why do they think up stories that link my name with yours?" Chip sang, and I thought of Andrea and that horrible note. "Why do the neighbors gossip all day behind their doors?" was my line. *Too much*. A lump rose in my throat.

I turned to sing my answering lines and my throat closed. No sound came out. I stopped, my hand on my throat, and looked toward Mr. Williams. He raised an eyebrow. "Cassie? What's the problem?"

"I don't know," I croaked. "Nothing will come out."

He bounced for a moment on the heels of his feet, thinking. "Maybe we've overworked your voice. Maybe you're under strain." He smiled and nodded to me. "Relax, Cassie. Chip, take Cassie into one of the practice rooms and show her some of those vocal relaxation exercises I taught you."

Chip and I climbed the stairs into an empty practice room. I slid onto the rickety piano stool, and Chip sat in a folding chair. There was an awkward silence.

"So what's wrong?" he finally said.

"I don't know." I couldn't look at him because

my eyes were filling with tears I couldn't stop. I turned toward the piano and absently played a chord.

"Well, I'm glad we have this time because I've been wanting to ask you what I did to make you mad." Chip wasn't looking at me, either. "I would have asked sooner, but I just couldn't do it."

I turned toward him. His face was red, and I couldn't believe what he had just said. "You thought I was mad at you?"

"Yeah. After everyone teased you about the dog show, then I heard you said—well, I figured you were mad at me because you were too embarrassed by what happened."

I shook my head. "No, I wasn't mad at you at all. You should have been mad at me."

"Why?"

"Because of that horrible note."

He looked out the tiny square window on the door at Mr. Williams and the chorus and took a deep breath: "Did you write it?"

"No, I didn't. Someone else did, someone who was jealous. But I wouldn't blame you if you were mad at me because I am guilty." My own cheeks were blushing, but I didn't care. I was going to confess everything. "I did mention to someone once that you smelled like onions one afternoon, but I didn't mean to hurt you and that was before I really knew you. I never dreamed it would go all through the school. I never meant to hurt you." My tears were flowing freely now, but it felt good to spill my guts and bring everything out into the open. "I'm really sorry, Chip."

Suddenly all the pain and fear of the last few weeks welled up inside and I really started to cry. He was my friend, he was the one person who had the courage to be honest with me, and I almost lost him and might still.

"*Shhh*, Cassie, don't cry," Chip whispered, glancing out the door again. "Mr. Williams will call for us in a few minutes, and you don't want to go out there all red-eyed."

He was right, so I hushed and tried to compose my face. When I was calm, Chip smiled. "It seems to me that we've just had a misunderstanding here. Let's forget all about it. Just one thing—" He looked at me sternly and I froze. "I promise I won't eat onions before rehearsals anymore."

"If you like them, you eat them." I smiled. "I'll bury my hamburgers in onions, too, and we'll *both* have onion breath!"

Through the thick rehearsal room door we heard the chorus stop singing. "Mr. Williams will be asking for us any minute," whispered Chip, "and you're not ready to go out there yet—your face is still kinda blotchy. Quick— bend over like you're going to touch your toes."

I did. I could feel the blood rushing to my face.

"Now hang your hands down and sing a scale—slowly."

I did. There was something relaxing about

singing upside-down, and the lump in my throat had dissolved. I felt much better. I looked over at upside-down Chip, whose face was red, too, and laughed.

When Mr. Williams opened the door and saw us singing scales with our rears in the air, he burst into laughter. That did it. Rehearsal was dismissed for the rest of the day, and Chip saved me from facing the entire group with my red eyes and puffy cheeks. And by the time he finished walking me home, I felt and looked 100 percent better.

13

Our first weekend at Dad's place was a disappointment. Sailing was out of the question because Dad had just moved into his new condo on the beach, and he needed both Saturday and Sunday to move boxes and put things away. Max and I were going to serve two purposes: we would help him unpack and fulfill his fatherly obligation at the same time.

We walked into the new peach and aqua condo and Dad beamed proudly. "Max, there's a supply of Twinkies for you in the cupboard. Cassie, there's a beautiful ocean view and lots of room to romp, and we'll order your favorite pizza for lunch! Now let's set up the new place."

Several of the packing boxes, I noticed, had come straight from Mom's house, as had several pieces of furniture. He must have officially moved out the day before while we were at school. I was glad I wasn't home for the battle of "who gets what."

He had a new bedroom suite, but our old dining room table. I recognized several battered unmatched pots and pans that had been Mom's, as well as a set of knives, forks, and spoons. I held up a familiar fork and made a face at Max. "Guess we'll be using the silver at Mom's house."

All of the computer stuff was here, of course, and in one box I found several baby pictures of me and Max. Dad made a big deal out of that box. "Oh, now those *are* important," he said, smiling. "Where should I put them? On my desk? By the telephone? Cassie, you can be the lady of the house and arrange things."

We ordered a pizza for lunch, and after it came we sat down amid the boxes and picnicked on the floor. "I hope you two like this place as much as I do," he said, sponging a drop of tomato sauce off his new carpet. "Just think— in the summer you can surf, fish, or just lie on the beach. Cassie, there's good shopping nearby, and you can meet your friends at the mall there if you like."

"It's great, Dad," I said, but without much enthusiasm.

When we finished Dad asked if I'd clean up while he and Max went down to the beach. "I promise I'll make Max clean up dinner." He winked, and before I could say anything, those two were out the door.

I finished cleaning up and took my first good

look around. I had been organizing the kitchen all morning, and I had to admit Dad had found a nice place. There was a balcony that opened up from the living room and overlooked the beach. A cool ocean breeze filled the room when the sliding door was open. *Maybe this won't be too bad,* I thought.

It was a three-bedroom condo, and I was surprised when I walked into the third bedroom. Dad had said that I would sleep on a rollaway in the bedroom with all the computer equipment, but in the third bedroom I found Max's bed, his dresser, and a suitcase with most of his clothes. Did this have something to do with their summer trip? I didn't understand.

It all became clear when Max came back from the beach with his now-familiar troubled expression. "Max, what's wrong?" I asked. "Did you get attacked by bathing beauties?"

He shook his head. "No."

"Then what is it?"

"I'm living here." His brown eyes were serious, and I could tell he felt helpless and confused. "Mom and Dad want me to live here, and you're going to live with Mom. That's what their lawyers worked out. They say it will be easier for Mom. They've already moved my stuff in."

"I know. I saw it." I slumped into Dad's new couch, an ugly overstuffed modern thing, the complete opposite of Mom's tailored sofa. So much for not upsetting our lives, too.

"Can they do that, Cassie? Can they just take

me out of one school and put me in another? Even though there are only two months of school left, Dad says he can't drive me over to the old school, and so I have to change now. Can he do that?"

I pulled him onto the couch beside me and gently stroked his hair. Poor kid. *Sure, they can do anything they want,* I thought, *because we're just kids.*

And then I was angrier than ever. If they wanted to take themselves away, fine, but they were taking away my brother. They were splitting us up. What a fool I had been, thinking that I could get Mom and Dad back together again. Now it wasn't just Dad who was missing, it was Max, too. I was going to lose my brother!

Who was going to look after the boy genius with no common sense? The next time he did an experiment with his Bunsen burner he'd forget to turn it off as always and burn this dumb condo down! Who would make sure he didn't OD on Twinkies? Who was going to remind him to keep the top on his ant farm? Who would eat his crummy algae cookies?

A tear ran down my cheek. Who would help me with my geometry? Who else was there to tell me I sang as good as Whitney Houston? What was I going to do without my kid brother?

14

Dad didn't come back for almost an hour. He'd
been jogging on the beach, and he came back
in dripping sweat and smiling. "Hey, you guys,"
he called casually, "what do you want to do
tonight? Just name it. Why don't you go through
the yellow pages there for a good restaurant and
let me know where you want to go when I get
out of the shower. Then we could go—what do
you think? Putt-putt golfing?"

The doorbell rang while he was showering,
and through the peephole I saw a red-haired
woman in a flaming pink bikini holding up a
set of keys. I opened the door.

"Oh!" she said, surprised. "I was expecting to
see Glen. Is he around?"

"He's in the shower," I said simply.

"Well, don't get him out," she giggled, "but
please give him these keys. I'm his next-door

neighbor, and we've agreed to keep an eye on each other's places when one of us has to go out of town. Just tell him I'll be back Monday, and I'll check in with him then."

She gave me the keys and giggled again. "You're as dark and cute as he is. You must be his daughter."

I didn't say anything, I just nodded.

"Well, I've got to be going. See you 'round." Her small bare feet padded down the carpeted hall.

Max looked up when I closed the door. "Don't tell me Dad's got a girlfriend—"

"I don't think so." I crinkled my nose. "I don't think she's his type."

Dad came into the room then, his hair still wet from the shower. He wore a new fluffy terry-cloth robe that I'd never seen before, and he was wearing a new gold neckchain. I stood back and gave him a good look. Though it was hard to picture him as anything but my dad, if I had never seen him before I'd think he was good-looking. He was in good shape, and his dark eyes sparkled with intelligence and fun. He had a bald spot, but with everything else he had going for him, who would care?

"Your neighbor dropped her keys over." I pointed to them on the table. "She said she'd be back Monday."

"Desiree." Dad grinned. "Isn't she the greatest? Everyone in this building is really great."

He came around and popped Max playfully

with his towel. "Have you decided what you want to do for supper?"

The phone rang, and Dad went into the kitchen to answer it.

"What do you want to do?" I asked Max.

"Nothing." He was still upset about moving in with Dad. "Can you imagine? I've got to live here now, next door to—" He shook his head and rolled his eyes. "Desiree."

We were quiet, and Dad's voice carried from the kitchen: "I'm sorry, babe, but tonight's out. I'm going to take the kids out for dinner."

He paused. "Yes, I want them to meet you, but not this week. Next week, maybe. OK, next week for sure. Put it on your calendar."

Whoever "babe" was answered.

"Me, too," said Dad. "'Bye."

Dad came back into the living room, all smiles. "Well, have we decided? Where are we going? Pizza? Mexican? Chinese?"

I turned my head to get a good look at Dad's hand. The wedding ring was gone.

When Dad and Max dropped me off at home—that is, Mom's house and my home, not Max's home anymore—I let myself in with my key. The house was dark except for one light in the living room where Mom was watching television on the couch. I saw her before she saw me; she was wiping her eyes and crying as though her heart would break.

"Hi, Mom," I called from the darkness of the hall. I recognized the theme song from "Wheel of Fortune."

"Oh, hi, honey," she managed to say. "This is such a sad movie I can't watch one minute more."

She pushed the remote control and the TV screen went blank. "Come on in and sit down. How was your weekend with Dad?"

"Fine." I sat in the wing chair facing her.

"Do you like his new place?"

"Yeah, it's OK. It has a nice view of the beach."

"Did he buy a lot of new stuff?"

"Some."

"I don't know where he got the money." She sniffed and blew her nose. "From what he told the judge you'd think he was as poor as a church mouse." She pulled her legs under her and leaned toward me. "What's your dad up to these days?"

"I don't know." The questions were beginning to annoy me. "Just the usual, I guess."

"What did you do all weekend?"

"We helped him unpack and just sat around. He took us out for Chinese food."

"Does Max have a nice room?"

"He seems to like it."

"Nice neighbors? Any new friends?"

"A few."

"Is your father dating anybody?"

Ah, here was the question she really wanted to know. I didn't know whether to tell her about the neighbor in the bikini, the "babe" on the telephone, or the hundreds of pretty women on the beach. I decided to keep my mouth shut.

"He didn't mention anybody."

110

She nodded. Her game of twenty questions was apparently over, but I had a few of my own.

"Mom . . ." I traced the design in the carpet with my toe, not sure how to ask. Finally I just blurted it out: "Why didn't you tell me Max was going to live with Dad?"

She was surprised. "Honey, I didn't think it would matter to you one way or the other. Your father and I have worked it out so that you and Max will be together on weekends. One weekend Max will come here, and the next weekend you'll go to your father's."

It seemed so clear and logical to her, but she didn't understand that it wasn't the weekends I wanted to spend with Max. I had always enjoyed being with Max at school, after school, at breakfast, and after dinner when we did our homework. Now we were as separated as if we lived in different states.

My stomach hurt, and I couldn't stand to be in the living room for one more minute. I pretended to yawn and stood to leave. "Boy, I'm tired," I mumbled. "I'm going to bed."

"Just a minute, honey." Mom caught me by the hand and looked into my eyes. "I'm not very strong right now," she said, her chin quivering, "and I need you to be strong for me. From now on it's going to be just you and me, kiddo, and I need you to hang in there and make it as easy as possible for both of us. OK? Can we work together?"

I knew what she was saying: *Don't mess up at*

school, she was telling me. *Be a good girl, study hard, keep your room clean, and don't give me any hassles. I just can't handle them now.*

I nodded. What else could I do? Mom was hurting, it was plain to see. No matter what she had or hadn't done, she had not wanted a divorce. Neither had I. Neither had Max. But Dad had—or had he? Had Mom driven him to it? Did he really have a choice?

The questions kept going around and around in my head as I walked to my room and leaned against the doorway. I was more tired than I could ever remember being. It was going to be impossible to be strong for Mom and me, too, so the smiling, scarlet dancer would have to vanish. I couldn't support her, my mom, and myself, too.

The next morning at school I walked into the choir room and found Mr. Williams sitting in his little office. "Mr. Williams, I'm afraid I'm going to have to back out of the production," I said simply. "Some things have come up, and I don't want to sing."

He nearly dropped his coffee cup. "Cassie Perkins, what are you saying?" he asked. Then he smiled. "Is this some sort of a joke? A late April Fool's joke?"

I shook my head. "No, I just can't do it. Andrea's my understudy, and she knows the part. She'll do fine."

The warning bell rang, and I turned and left.

I didn't tell anyone, but apparently Mr. Williams did. At lunch Andrea lit into me.

"Are you *crazy*?" Andrea shrieked, causing at least ten heads to turn in our direction.

113

"What's wrong with you? Are you dying from cancer? Moving out of state? Or simply insane? Why would you give up your part in the musical?"

I shrugged. "I just don't care anymore, that's all. It's too much work, and I don't want to do it."

"You know who you sound like?" Andrea was glaring at me now. "You sound like Mandi. She doesn't care about anything either, at least not if it's something that takes a little work or a little commitment. She even dropped off the cheerleading squad because she said it was too much work and she wanted to spend more time with her new boyfriend."

"That's stupid, Andrea. It's not like that with me. You don't understand."

Andrea shook her head slowly and spoke to the empty chair next to her. "Is she crazy? Yes, she must be. With only two weeks until the performance, she backs out. And who does she tap as her replacement? Me!"

I didn't think she was very funny. "You're my understudy, and you know the part. You can do it."

"I may know the part, but I don't have half the voice you have, Cassie! I could practice from now until Christmas and never sing it as well as you could!"

I took a big bite of whatever it was they were feeding us. Hash or something. "I'm sorry," I mumbled with my mouth full of food, not even caring about my manners. "But break a leg, Andrea, here's your big break in show business."

Chip cornered me as soon as school was out. I had dreaded talking to him and had successfully avoided him all day in school. But now I couldn't. I liked him too much to run away, and I knew he deserved an answer.

"Let's go somewhere and talk."

"You should be getting to rehearsal," I reminded him, afraid to look up. "Only two weeks until the big show, you know."

"Mr. Williams will understand if I'm a little late."

We walked toward a big oak tree that stood outside the library window. I had often looked up at it when I was in the library, but I had never stood under it. Its size was overwhelming, and I felt dizzy when I looked up.

We sat on the polished roots that grew up out of the grass. "OK," Chip said, putting down his books and pulling out a long stalk of grass. "I'm your partner, and I have a right to know. Why did you quit the show?"

"I just wanted to."

"That's no reason."

"Yes, it is."

"No, it isn't. I don't want to get up and go to school on lots of mornings, but I do it anyway. You've got enough discipline to do things you don't feel like doing."

I searched for another reason. "Months ago, I

wanted to be in this show more than anything in the world. I wanted to show my parents and my friends what I could do, and I wanted to find out for myself what I could do."

"And you were doing great! So why don't you want that anymore?"

"I just don't care anymore."

"You cared last week—why don't you care today?"

I shrugged. "A girl has a right to change her mind."

"Don't give me that line." He shook his head in disgust.

"OK, I don't care because I don't need to prove it anymore. I know what I can do. My friends, most of them anyway, know what I can do."

"What about your parents? Do they know?"

"They don't care."

"Why not?"

I took a deep breath and let him have the full story: "Because they're divorcing, and they don't care about anything anymore except themselves. Dad's out being playboy of the century, and Mom's home every night wallowing in her own pity party. They took Max away, and they don't care what they're doing to me."

The words came out quickly, more than I had ever intended to tell him. I sounded irrational even to myself, but I couldn't stop the feelings.

"Why should I give them a surprise and

something nice when they don't deserve it? Sometimes I hate them!" I stood up and gave the gnarly tree root a kick. The root didn't budge, but I nearly broke my foot.

I cried then, partly from pain, partly from embarrassment. The more I cried, the worse I felt. Here I stood, crying like a baby in the school yard in front of the boy I liked more than anyone.

Chip seemed to understand. He stood up and took my hand. "Come on, let's walk," he said. "You don't want everyone in the library looking out here."

Something calmed me down, whether it was the walking or Chip's hand in mine, I didn't know. He waited until I had stopped crying to speak.

"You don't think anyone cares about what happens to you?"

"No, I don't. Mandi was right; she told me that her parents stopped caring for her when they stopped caring for each other, and I can see it happening in our family, too. They just want me to be good and stay out of their hair. They don't care, and I don't care, either."

"You're wrong." Chip's voice was steady and quiet. "Your parents do care, but they're too wrapped up in their own hurt to let you know how much they care. Your friends care about you and so does Mr. Williams. No one wants you to quit the play."

Chip stopped walking and looked me steadily in the eye. "I care about you a lot. And God cares about you very much."

I snorted. "God cares? If God cares about me so much, why did he make all this stuff happen?"

Chip shook his head. "God doesn't make bad things happen, people do. I don't know why your parents split up. Maybe they don't even know why." We started walking again, and Chip spoke slowly: "My parents split up two years ago, and it was the worst time of my life."

I couldn't believe it. Mr. and Mrs. Charming had split up? They seemed so in love! "What happened?" I blurted out. "I didn't even want to tell you about my parents because I thought you'd never understand. Your parents are so perfect together!"

Chip shrugged. "I don't know what happened to make them split, but they fought all the time and Dad moved out. About six months later, when the divorce would have been final, he came home, brought Mother flowers, and told her that he wasn't going to give up on their marriage. They went to a counselor for help, and Dad told me he learned that love isn't a feeling, it's a commitment."

"Like a promise," I whispered. "Love is a promise."

"I guess so," Chip answered. "Dad says he knows now that real love isn't something that goes away or turns sour. Marriage is like the ultimate promise, and if you live every day determined to keep your promise to love, it changes your attitude. Anyway, my parents worked their problems out, and whenever they

118

have a disagreement now, they pray about their problem. I never hear them fight anymore."

"How?" I asked softly.

"How what?" Chip was confused.

"How did your dad learn all this stuff? What made him so smart all of a sudden?"

Chip smiled at me. "From church, I guess. Dad says he realizes that God gave us the greatest example of love. He promised to love us and he does, even when we act terrible and don't love him back. But God keeps his promises."

It sounded like the fairy-tale ending I would have expected from Chip's parents. But my mopey mother and playboy father weren't about to learn any lessons or get back together. Our family hadn't been inside a church in years, and I didn't think my parents would look for answers in a church, anyway. A rock sat in our path and I gave it a good kick.

"So why are you taking everything out on that poor rock?" Chip asked.

I looked at him in disbelief. "Didn't you hear what my parents have done to me and Max? Wouldn't you be angry, too?"

"Probably. But you can't stay mad at them forever."

"Oh, yes I can."

"But Cassie, it isn't worth it. Just look at yourself—you're mad and stiff, and your face is red. You're no fun, and by quitting the play you're losing the thing you enjoy most."

"I'm no fun?" Now I was mad at Chip.

119

"No," he laughed. "But you used to be. And you can be again if you'll just stop being angry. Forgive your parents and get on with your life."

"How can you talk?" I stopped walking and turned on him. "Your parents are perfect now—they got back together. Mine are splitting forever! Dad has a girlfriend! You don't know what I'm going through. Everyone around me has broken their promises to me, and my parents have simply quit! Parents are supposed to be there forever!"

"Nobody's perfect," Chip said quietly. "And God is the only one who never breaks a promise. If you can't accept that people will sometimes let you down, you'll only be hurting yourself. Don't you ever make a mistake or break a promise?"

I bit my lip. "Yeah, sometimes," I confessed. "But I've never messed up as bad as my parents have."

"You might sometime," Chip said gently. "And when you do, you'll know how good it feels to be forgiven. So think about forgiving your parents now."

We walked on in silence, and I remembered how embarrassed I had been when my comments about Chip's onion breath had gone all around school. I had felt *terrible*, and Chip was right, it felt wonderful to hear him say, "It's OK, I forgive you."

But I was shaking inside, I was so angry and confused. Chip was right. I should get over my

anger and get on with life as usual. If I stayed
mad, all that anger would eat me up, just like
Dad always said it would.

So I knew I ought to forgive Mom and Dad.
But I couldn't. Not yet.

16

I spent the rest of that week in a fog. Chip's words kept echoing in my mind, *God is the only one who never breaks a promise.* I hated to admit he was right, but I knew he was. And there was another thought that kept bouncing around in my brain—did God really, truly, forever-and-always love me?

None of those thoughts made sense, but being angry did. I wasn't mad at Max anymore, but he broke a promise the time he didn't bring the stuff for my throat. I wasn't mad at Andrea anymore, either, and she broke a *big* promise when she told about Chip and the onions. But I was still really mad at Mom and Dad. "In fact," I whispered under my breath as my dad drove away on Friday night, "I might be mad at you forever." Why couldn't I forgive my parents for not staying together?

It was Max's weekend at our house. When Dad dropped him off I could tell Max felt uncomfortable. He didn't know where to go—his room had been emptied, and his beloved gerbils, algae, and outfits were at Dad's.

Mom made a point of being home when Max was dropped off. "Max, honey, it's so good to see you," she whispered as she hugged him. I guess I wasn't the only one who noticed how quiet the house was without the whiz kid around to liven things up.

"Honey, I'm afraid you'll have to sleep on the couch tonight," Mom told him as she carried his overnight bag in from the garage. "We'll go out tomorrow and find a bed for you somewhere. Maybe I can find an inexpensive one in the classified section or at a yard sale."

She took Max's bag into his room and I whispered, "You're lucky—you don't get a rollaway." Max laughed. "How are ya doin', kiddo?" I looked in his shirt pocket. "What, no gerbils?"

"Nope. No wildlife at all, just me."

"That's wildlife enough."

His eyes told me he was glad to be home. "We'll talk later," I promised, "but Mom will grill you first."

Sure enough, Mom played twenty questions with Max, too, but when she asked if Dad was dating anybody, Max nodded and said, "Sure. Julie Smith."

Mom's smile froze. "Julie Smith? Who is she,

someone he picked up at a swinging singles coffee shop?"

"No, Mom, she's nice," Max said calmly. "She's a science writer at NASA."

I was dying to hear all about this Julie, but Mom didn't want to hear any more. "Let's go," she said, abruptly gathering her purse and keys. "I've planned a special dinner for both of you." A smile was plastered on her face, but it didn't reach her eyes. "Just remember not to break my budget."

Later, after Mom had gone to bed, I tiptoed into the living room where Max was stretched out on the couch watching reruns of "Murder She Wrote" and taking notes on the clues. "Throw me down a pillow, Max," I said, stretching out on the floor beside him, "and tell me all about Julie."

Max shrugged. "I've only met her once. She's very nice, very intelligent, and very pretty. She came over to dinner the other night, and she and Dad worked on a project for the shuttle orbiter."

"Have they been working together a long time?"

"I don't know. Why?"

"Never mind. I just wondered how long he has known her."

"I don't know."

"Is he going to marry her?"

Max was irritated. "How should I know? Ask him yourself."

"What do you call her?"

"Who?"

"Julie."

"I don't call her anything. She hasn't been around long enough."

"What does Dad call her?"

Max smirked. "You wouldn't believe it."

"Try me."

"Babe."

"He calls her *babe?*"

"Yeah, but only when they think I'm not around."

So Julie Smith was the mysterious woman on the phone. Julie Smith was the woman Dad wanted us to meet.

"I think Dad's serious about this woman."

"How would you know?"

"Female intuition."

Max snorted. "Women's intuition has absolutely no scientific basis in fact."

"Mine does."

"Anyway, who cares? If he wants to get serious with Julie, that's fine with me."

"How can you say that?" For a whiz kid, he could be so dense! "If he marries someone else, he can't marry Mom again! And if Mom and Dad don't get back together, are you ready to have a stepmother?"

"I don't think of it that way, I think of her as Dad's girlfriend who might be his wife. You don't live there, Cassie; you don't know that Dad is no housekeeper. He really needs someone to help around the house. He's already leaving dirty dishes for you to clean next weekend."

"Gross! I don't believe it!"

"Don't worry, there aren't that many dishes because Dad can't cook, either, so we eat out a lot."

"Max, you dummy, men don't get married just so they can have a woman to clean their houses!"

"Why do they get married, then?"

"They're supposed to be in love. They're supposed to be friends."

Max shook his head. "What's love? An emotional response with no basis in fact or logic."

I had heard this before. "Love's supposed to be based on a promise, a commitment."

Max shrugged. "Since people are illogical and unstable creatures—" He paused and scratched his head, realizing, I knew, that he was neither illogical nor unstable. "Well, since *most* people are illogical and unstable, promises are often broken. Anyway, I don't worry about Dad. I have other things to think about."

"What other things?" I could just envision Max on the beach, surrounded by twenty-year-old beauties who were using him to get their income tax forms done or their solar water heaters repaired. "What's keeping you busy these days?"

Max sat up, Indian style, and looked at me. "I just decided to approach the whole thing scientifically. It didn't make sense to spend energy wishing or crying or whining, although I did a lot of that at first."

For a moment there was a flicker of the little boy in those brown eyes, but then he vanished, and logical Max was back in his place. "I was confused at first, but since then I've just learned to ignore whatever Mom and Dad are doing. I'm going to concentrate on my own efforts to help the world." He pointed his pencil at me and leaned forward to whisper, "I'm going to discover the cure for cancer."

How like Max. While he rattled on about killer T cells and suppressor T cells, I wondered how he could separate himself from all that was going on around him. Maybe he was just hiding what he really felt.

"Max," I interrupted, "are you mad at Mom and Dad?"

"Why should I be?"

"Because they hurt you! Because they let our home disappear! They ruined our lives, for heaven's sake!"

"No, they didn't ruin our lives. You're the same as you were before the divorce and so am I. We're in different places and we have different problems, but we're the same people, Cassie. At least I am."

He looked at me closely. "Aren't you?"

Suki came over and lay beside me. I put my arm around her and thought hard. "I don't know. I don't know if I want to be."

Max shrugged and turned toward the television.

Angela Lansbury had found the murderer on "Murder She Wrote," and Max checked his notes. "Very predictable," he murmured. "Really an obvious choice."

I sighed and stood up. "Good night, Max. But if you really want to change the world, I know something that needs a cure far worse than cancer."

"What?" His eyes gleamed with interest.

"Divorce. Cure that, and you'll change the world."

"You can't cure divorce." He was talking down to me again, like I was the child and he was the oldest. "People decide to get divorced, they don't decide to get cancer. And you can die from cancer, but you can't die from divorce."

"It can make you feel like you're dead."

"That doesn't last forever." Max's brown eyes were more serious than I had ever seen them. He looked like a thirty-year-old man smiling through the face of a kid. "You can get better if you want to."

"Maybe," I said as I turned to leave. "In a couple hundred years."

Before I went to sleep, I opened my private note-book and tried to write a poem for Chip:

> *Because you cared,*
> *Because you dared,*
> *Because you—*

Stared? Fared? Prepared? "Forget it," I muttered to myself. "I'm too tired to think tonight." As I flipped a page, I saw my poem for the astronauts:

> *The early twilight settles around the world—*
> *The silv'ry hush wraps itself around the earth.*
> *I sit missing you.*
> *The morning rain steadily drips from rooftops.*
> *The buzz of the cricket adds to morning song.*
> *My heart sings of you.*

The cool evening breeze fingers my hair and cheek.
The sweet day is closing and nighttime has come.
But you are not home.
—Cassie Perkins, age 13.

Brother! I felt like I had aged ten years since I wrote that poem. I ripped the page out of the notebook, crumpled it, and tossed it under my bed. How sappy could I get? Now I couldn't even remember what I felt for the astronauts who were gone because Dad was gone, and Max was gone every weekday and every other weekend.

That night I dreamed it was Christmas morning. Mom, Dad, Max, and I were gathered around a Christmas tree so tall that we cut a hole in the ceiling just to stand it upright. I was wearing a satin scarlet gown and sequined ballet slippers. They were gorgeous!

Dad was dressed in a red Santa suit handing out presents. Max opened his; it was a shoebox filled with Twinkies. On a tiny card attached to one Twinkie was a note: "The cure for cancer." Max was overjoyed; he had known it all along.

Dad handed Mom a box, and she smiled like she used to years ago. "Why, Glen," she laughed merrily, "this box is empty. You've given me nothing!" But she laughed and laughed like it was the best gift in the world, and I couldn't understand why.

Dad handed me a large box, and when I opened it at first I couldn't see anything. But

there at the bottom was Dad's wedding ring
with lots of loopy purple ribbons tied around it.
"Wear it as an earring," he said. "I have no use
for it."

"But Dad," I tried to explain, "I can't wear
your ring as an earring. I don't want to lose it!"

Dad smiled. "Don't worry. It doesn't matter if
it is here today and gone tomorrow."

"But it matters to me!" I yelled, but no one
heard. They all got up and began to square
dance, Mom with Max and Dad with Suki. It
was so weird, but they were laughing and dancing and having a great time while I just sat there
in my scarlet gown crying harder and harder. I
began to sob, and then I woke myself up, clutch-
ing my stomach and sobbing.

Suki was awake and watching me, her head
cocked to one side. "How could you?" I asked
her furiously. "How could you get up and dance
without me?" Then the utter silliness of the
dream hit me, and I pulled Suki into my arms
and hugged her tight. It had all been so stupid,
but it was true. Life was dancing by, and I was
crying on the sidelines, alone.

Did anyone really care? Could anyone really
help? Chip's words were still in my head, so
with tears in my eyes and Suki by my side, I
looked toward the ceiling. "God," I whispered,
"if you're up there and you really do love me,
help me get my life back—please." Nothing
happened—nothing changed. But I had never

really talked to God before, and I certainly had never asked for anything.

I snuggled back under my blanket and closed my eyes. Maybe if I assured him that I believed that he'd help. "God—," I whispered again, "thanks."

The next Monday morning I was back in Mr. Williams' office. "Mr. Williams—" I gulped. "I'd like my part back in the musical. I know I've missed a week of rehearsals, but I can make it up."

Mr. Williams looked stern. He wanted to give me the part, I knew, but he might decide not to, just to teach me a lesson about quitting. I held my breath.

"Young lady, the part is not mine to give," he said finally. "Andrea Milford has the part, and it will be up to her to decide what to do. It wouldn't be fair to just take it from her on your whim."

I nodded. "You're right, sir. I'll ask her."

"No," Mr. Williams said, shaking his head. "She might feel pressure from you because you're her friend. I'll ask her if she'd be willing to give up the solo parts. If she agrees, you're back in."

I saw Andrea at lunch, and it was hard not to mention to her that I wanted back in the production. Mr. Williams hadn't spoken to her yet, and Andrea didn't even mention the musical. Last week I had made it clear enough I considered the subject closed.

But after school when the bell rang and rehearsals had begun, I waited out of sight outside the choir room just in case Andrea wanted to keep the part. I didn't want to go in there and have to leave again because I was out to stay. *You've made your bed,* I could hear my mother say, *now lie in it.*

But after a few minutes Andrea stepped out the door, and I knew she was going to find me. "Andrea!" I called.

"There you are!" She was smiling. "Of course you can have your part back! But you'll have to admit you were stupid—just think, you missed an entire week of rehearsals with Chip!"

I was so relieved and so happy that I hugged her, and there we stood, like a couple of grinning fools. When we stepped into the choir room, the entire group applauded. It was embarrassing, and I wanted to sink into the floor. "We're glad you're back," said Mr. Williams, smiling, and Chip stepped forward, bowed, and said, "May I have this dance, Miss Laurie?"

"Not until I get into my costume!" I ran toward the girls' dressing room. No more sidelines for this dancer.

18

That Friday night our school cafeteria was filled with parents and friends. The tables had been folded and put away, and rows of chairs filled the huge room. At the front of the room a makeshift curtain had been strung, and from behind it, I could see on the tile floor the rows of masking tape that defined our "stage." Several bales of hay had been set on the floor as boundaries and places for singers to sit during the performance.

I had a million butterflies in my stomach. Peeping out through the heavy curtain, I could see that Mom was there with Max, and on his shirt he wore a button that said, "My sister is Cassie Perkins." He had called Mom and officially asked if he could escort her to the performance. It was a pretty classy move, I had to admit. I would never have thought of it, but I could tell now that Mom was proud. I don't think I could have gotten her to come alone, and I realized my old dream of having Mom and Dad sit together was pretty farfetched.

I could see Mom holding the note I had left for her on the kitchen table. "Mom," I had written, "please come to the school production tonight at 7:00. Max will escort you, and I have a special surprise for you. P.S. I love you."

Dad and his date were sitting in the other section of seats. I assumed the dark-haired lady sitting next to him was Julie Smith. They were deep in conversation, their heads only inches apart. It was strange to see them together, but I tried to look at them with Max's analytical eyes. Yes, she was pretty in a refined way, not all flash and glitter. Yes, Dad looked happy. Those little furrows of worry I had seen in his forehead months ago had been erased. He looked younger somehow. But I couldn't think about them together, not yet. I just wasn't ready to dwell on what might happen in the future. I was having a hard enough time getting through the present—and this night!

But he was holding his note, too. I had sent his with Max and had written pretty much the same message: "Dear Dad: Please come to our school production tonight at 7:00. I love you and I have a special surprise for you. Always, your Gypsy Girl."

"Come away from the curtain!" Mr. Williams' intense backstage whisper stirred up my butterflies again, and I stopped peeking at the audience

138

and tried to concentrate on what I was doing. First came "Oklahoma!", then my song with Chip, then came my solo with the girls' chorus, then we would all do our square-dance number to "The Surrey with the Fringe on the Top."

"You all look great," Mr. Williams whispered as we huddled around him. "Now I know you'll do fine, so if you're thinking about getting nervous, just forget it."

He looked a lot more confident than I felt, and I noticed even Andrea seemed a shade paler than usual. She felt me looking at her, and when her eyes met mine, she flashed me a grin. "Break a leg!" she mouthed the words across the crowd, and I whispered back, "You, too!"

Mr. Williams looked at his watch and smiled. "We've got three minutes until the curtain goes up. I want you to find a partner, tell that person he's worked hard and he's going to do *great,* then get to your places. Go!"

I turned in confusion and nearly bumped into Chip, but he grabbed both my hands and steadied me. "Cassie, you've worked very hard and you're going to be *fantastic!*" The warmth of his hands calmed the butterflies in my stomach, and I felt my cheeks reddening.

But I was absolutely on top of the world. "Chip, you've worked real hard and you're going to be incredible," I told him. "Everything is going to be super." I had to look down a minute; the smile in those blue eyes was enough to make me forget every word I'd memorized.

139

"And thanks, you know, for being there when I needed you. You were right, and I'd be stupid to stay mad at the world forever. I'm ready to get on with my life, and I even asked God to help out."

Chip smiled and pulled me to our starting marks. We posed in our starting position, and I could see the curtain parting and the beaming audience behind it. "Everything is going to be great!" I whispered in his ear. "I promise!"

And I knew it was the truth.

*If you've enjoyed the **Cassie Perkins** books,
you'll want to read these additional series from
Tyndale House Publishers!*

Anika Scott

These fascinating stories of an American girl growing up in
Africa encourage young readers to build a Christian worldview.

#1 The Impossible Lisa Barnes

#2 Tianna the Terrible

#3 Anika's Mountain

#4 Ambush at Amboseli

#5 Sabrina the Schemer

Elizabeth Gail

Through her foster parents, Elizabeth Gail finds love,
acceptance, and Christ's healing as she matures from a
likeable girl to an admirable woman. Join her for 21 exciting
adventures, including these latest releases:

#20 The Mystery of the Hidden Key

#21 The Secret of the Gold Charm

You can find Tyndale books at fine bookstores everywhere.
If you are unable to find these titles at your local bookstore,
you may write for ordering information to:

**Tyndale House Publishers
Tyndale Family Products Dept.
Box 448
Wheaton, IL 60189**